LASSIE
Lost in the Snow

LASSIE
Lost in the Snow

Steve Frazee

A TARGET BOOK

published by
the Paperback Division of
W. H. ALLEN & Co. Ltd

A Target Book
Published in 1978
by the Paperback Division of W. H. Allen & Co. Ltd
A Howard and Wyndham Company
44 Hill Street, London W1X 8LB

First published in 1969 in the U.S.A.
by Western Publishing Company, Inc.

Published by arrangement with
Western Publishing Company, Inc.,
Racine, Wisconsin, U.S.A.

Printed in Great Britain by
Hunt Barnard Printing Ltd,
Aylesbury, Bucks

ISBN 0 426 20012 8

Contents

Chapter 1

TRICKED

It was Scott Turner's first experience with a snowmobile, so he was taking it easy, trying to learn all he could about the vehicle here in the foothills, where the snow was only eighteen inches deep.

At first Lassie had wanted nothing to do with the noisy machine. When Pete Bartholomew, the district ranger, started the engine in the Forest Service garage back in Gateway, Lassie had jumped up and scooted out of the place as if her own tail were on fire.

In the open, however, the sound of the busy engine did not bother her. With her gold and white coat gleaming in the sun, she was riding in the sled trailer, looking as if she owned the whole Wapiti National Forest.

When Scott stopped at the foot of a steep hill, Lassie barked a protest at the delay.

Letting the engine idle, Scott got off the seat to study the country ahead. Here on the sunny slopes, the snow had settled considerably, but he knew it would be much deeper on the shady side of the hills beyond.

Lassie barked again, as if to say, 'Come on! Let's get going, driver!'

Scott's young, good-natured features broke into a grin. 'Relax. You'll get plenty of riding before the afternoon is over.'

Behind them lay the long scrawl of tracks the snowmobile had made from where Scott had left the jeep and trailer, two miles away. The wide, cleated traction belt had not sunk very far into the snow. So far it had been very easy going.

Scott looked across the valley at the Menzies Mountains, great peaks that stretched across the sky, north and south for a hundred miles. The wedge tops of the mountains were starkly grey and bare, but the snow was deep in the troughs of the high slopes.

According to Pete Bartholomew, it was twelve to fifteen feet deep in the timber and in the narrow valleys that led into the mountains.

Almost all of that vast expanse, from the plunging summits of the peaks to far down in the piñon foothills, was part of the Sawatch District of the Wapiti National Forest.

A few years before, probably not ten people would have visited it in winter, but times had changed. Now there were snowmobiles. The great white wilderness was now visited by hundreds of people, who went in winter where even jeeps could not go in summer.

Snowmobiling was a tremendous sport. More and more people were being attracted to it every winter. They were having fun, but they were also creating some serious problems, and that was the reason Scott Turner had come to the Sawatch District two days after Christmas.

Lassie barked again, but this time it was not an impatient bark; it was a warning signal. She was looking towards a ridge on the left. A few moments later Scott heard the whirring sound of engines.

The noise increased. *Snowmobiles*, Scott thought. *The drivers really have their engines revved up.*

He stared in astonishment when he saw two blue snowmobiles hit the crest of the ridge. Then, side by side, they shot into the air. The two skis of the front running gear of each machine seemed to be reaching, stretching to outdo the other vehicle.

They sailed for about fifteen feet. Scott expected to see them go end over end in a crash, but they hit the downslope at full tilt, bounced a little, and went roaring on down the hill, the drivers yelling like triumphant Indians.

'Wow!' Scott muttered. That sort of thing was pretty wild. He could see himself trying a jump like that and going one way while the machine went in another direction.

The drivers made a fast, leaning turn at the bottom of the hill. Then they saw Scott and Lassie and headed up towards them.

A moment later a huge husky came sailing over the ridge in a cloud of snow, leaping in tremendous bounds on the trail of the blue snowmobiles.

As the two drivers came closer, Scott stared in amazement. They were *boys*, not more than twelve or thirteen years old, wearing dark Cossack hats and red nylon jackets!

Racing their machines on an angling ascent, they were coming so fast that Scott thought they were going to crash into him. So did Lassie. Growling her disapproval, she leaped from the trailer and floundered through the snow to get out of the way.

Scott was ready to make a quick jump himself, but the boys stopped their machines a few feet short of him and said, almost in unison, 'Hi!'

'Hi, yourselves. What *are* you guys, Olympic ski

jumpers?' They were twins, he decided – snub-nosed, blond, and suntanned – the hot rod twins.

'Aw, that wasn't much of a jump,' one of them said. 'You want to try it with us?'

Scott grinned. 'No, thanks!'

The big husky came plunging towards them. Lassie's hair stood up, and she growled.

'Easy, girl,' Scott said.

'Chinook won't hurt her,' one of the twins assured him.

Lassie jumped back into the trailer. Wagging his bushy tail, Chinook tried to make friends with her, but she kept warning him away from her sled, as if to say, 'This is mine, you big monster!'

'They'll get along.' Scott chuckled. 'What are you boys doing out of school?'

'Christmas vacation!'

'Sure; I forgot.'

The twins studied Scott's snowmobile closely. 'That old green Snow Rocket is a Forest Service job,' one of them declared. 'Rope starter, eighteen-inch track, hard to turn. Pretty slow. It's got lots of power, though.'

The other boy patted the fibre-glass cowling of his machine. 'You Forest Service guys ought to get Skimmers like ours. Then you could catch somebody, if you had to.'

'We're not much interested in catching anyone,' Scott said. 'What gave you that idea?'

'I thought the Forest Service was talking about keeping snowmobiles out of the mountains if they didn't do just what you said.'

'Is that the talk around this area?'

The boy shrugged. 'I guess so.'

'Someone has the wrong idea, then. So far as I

know, the Forest Service has no plans to shut off the national forests to snowmobiles.'

Scott was on the verge of making a little speech, but then he thought better of it and directed the conversation towards getting acquainted with the twins.

Their names were Bob and Ted Pettigrew. Their home was on the outskirts of Gateway, and their father was Fritz Pettigrew, the Skimmer dealer. *No wonder they were so enthusiastic about the blue snowmobiles,* Scott thought.

He watched Chinook trying to be friendly with Lassie. She had quit growling at him, but she still bared her teeth each time he tried to get close to the trailer.

'We've got to go home pretty soon,' Bob said. 'You want to make a jump with us – just a little one?'

'This is my first time on a snowmobile. I don't think I want to try any jumps yet.' Scott paused. 'Isn't that sort of thing a little hard on the machines?'

'Not too bad,' Ted said, 'if you land right.'

'Does your dad know you do that?'

The twins looked at each other. 'He does it sometimes when he's demonstrating a Skimmer, just to show people how tough they are,' Bob said. He grinned. 'Maybe he doesn't know how *far* we try to jump.'

The boys got on their Skimmers. 'We're going to take one more run,' Ted said. 'You want to come along, Ranger?'

'I'll give it a try.'

Chinook hurried to get on the seat behind Ted.

'How can he stick on that seat?' Scott asked.

'He falls off on the turns sometimes, but that doesn't bother him. He likes snow.'

Before the twins revved up their engines, they exchanged glances. Scott was aware of their quick look. *They'll lure me over a jump, if they can,* he told himself. He followed them up the hill.

Driving in the track of the blue Skimmers, Scott discovered that he could go as fast as the lighter machines on the steep incline. They walked away from him quickly, however, on the other side of the ridge as they wove in and out of the piñons and junipers on the sidehill.

The fun of the thing soon took hold of him. It was great to churn along at fifteen miles an hour, though it seemed much faster. He looked back at Lassie. She, too, was enjoying the ride.

He caught up with the boys when they stopped to let Chinook back on after he had fallen off on a turn in soft snow.

For ten minutes Scott followed the twins up and down the rolling hills, along the sides of the slopes, in and out of the trees.

They dipped down close to the bottom of a shaded, snow-filled gulch and went along beside it for a hundred yards. Then the twins plunged into a stand of junipers. Needles flew from some of the branches as the snowmobiles skinned through.

Scott cut his speed down. He had to duck low limbs going through the trees. Suddenly he was out of the thicket. Too late he saw that the boys had made a sharp uphill turn under full power.

He pulled the steering bar of the Rocket hard to the right, but the skis were slow to respond. The machine went on past the turn. Then he began to slide toward the gulch. He let up on the gas.

Half buried in fluffy snow, he came to a stop, with the Rocket angled uphill. He was still upright, and so was the sled, but the sled had skidded sideways. It was full of snow. Lassie was standing, shaking herself in disgust.

The twins, grinning like happy imps, were watching from a short distance uphill.

'You should have gunned it wide open on the turn!' Bob yelled.

They trapped me on that one rather neatly, Scott thought. The engine was still idling. Now he gave it more gas, and for a moment he thought it was going to pull out.

There was plenty of power, but suddenly it became digging power that settled him lower in the coarse-crystalled snow. He let up on the gas.

'I think you're stuck!' Ted yelled.

Without thinking, Scott stepped off the snowmobile to size up the situation. He sank to his waist. Lassie apparently thought he was going to walk out, and she jumped out of the snow-filled trailer. She struck with a *plop!* and disappeared.

By the time Scott wallowed over to her, she had pawed her way up and was trying to swim to something solid.

Pulling Lassie with him, Scott struggled back to the machine. Something bumped against his legs, and there was Chinook. The snow didn't seem to bother him. In powerful surges the big husky led the way back to where the twins had made the turn. Scott gave Lassie a heave, and she followed Chinook over to the broken trail.

It took Scott ten minutes of struggling in the deep snow to manhandle the Rocket and the sled around so that they were parallel with the gulch.

'He's not so dumb,' Bob told his brother. 'He

knows he can't come straight up the hill from a standing start.'

'It *was* sort of a dirty trick we played on him, wasn't it?'

'Not too bad. We can tow him out if he slides all the way into the gulch.'

Scott gave the snowmobile gas by slowly squeezing the hand lever on the steering bar. The traction belt dug in, and he slid a little closer to the gulch.

Then the machine crawled ahead and began to gain speed. He gave it full throttle, steering towards a gradual ascent of the hill. With no more difficulty, he drove up to the top of the hill and swung back to a stop between the twins.

They brought the Skimmers up, with Lassie and Chinook digging along behind.

'Well?' Scott said.

The boys gave him sheepish looks, then glanced away. 'We said those old Rockets had lots of power, didn't we?' Bob asked.

'So you did.' Scott nodded. He pointed towards the gulch. 'How far could you walk in snow like that?'

'Not very far,' Ted said. 'Of course, we don't get stuck. You really ought to have snowshoes.'

'Where are yours?'

'I said we never get stuck.'

'We'd better get home.' As Ted started away, Chinook leaped on behind him, bracing himself with everything but his tail.

From the ridge Scott watched the boys race down the hill and skim out on the flats. Ted made no sharp turns, and Chinook stayed on.

Lassie whined as she watched the Skimmers grow smaller.

'You sort of liked Chinook, didn't you – especially

after he came down in the deep snow to help you?'

The collie gave a little bark, as if to agree. She was not anxious to get back into the trailer, even after Scott brushed the snow out of it. He did not try to force her, but let her follow along in the track as he tested the Rocket some more.

Though the snow on the sunny slope made firm going for the machine, Lassie's small feet and slender legs kept punching through it. Unlike Chinook, she was just not built for snow travel. The second time Scott stopped, Lassie jumped into the trailer.

He made several more short runs through the deep, soft snow on the north slopes. Each time he made Lassie wait on top of the main ridge. After two more hours, Scott felt that he had learned at least a few things about a snowmobile.

The first big lesson was that one should never go into deep snow without skis or snowshoes.

On the easy two-mile run back to the Jeep, he whirred along at about twenty miles an hour. He wondered how long it would take him and Lassie to walk that same distance through the foot and a half of snow.

Chapter 2

DISAGREEMENT

It was only a small group who met that night in the district ranger's office to discuss the problems being caused by snowmobiles.

After introducing Scott to the gathering, Pete Barthomolew said, 'Now, Scott, here, doesn't claim to have all the answers or even to know much about snowmobiling.

'In fact, he made his first run this afternoon in the North Hills, and the way I get it, he managed to bury himself and Lassie.'

'So I heard.' Fritz Pettigrew laughed. He was a tall man with crew-cut sandy hair. 'Someone should have warned him about my boys.'

Scott smiled. 'I know about them now.' Then he grew serious. 'Some estimates say that there are about four hundred thousand snowmobiles in the country, with more coming all the time. In Pete's district there are one hundred and sixty-three – '

'One sixty-five,' Jim Benton said. 'I sold two more this morning.' He was a jolly-looking round-faced man, the Glory snowmobile dealer.

'I guess I'll have to sell four tomorrow then,' Pettigrew said. 'Sorry, Mr Turner, we won't interrupt again.'

'Snowmobiles are creating problems for a lot of agencies,' Scott went on. 'I want to emphasise, first off, that the Forest Service doesn't want to be forced into making a lot of stiff regulations about snowmobiles in the national forests.

'It could come to that, but we want to avoid it if at all possible. We'd much prefer that snowmobilers work out codes of behaviour and enforce them through their own clubs.

'This evening I'd like to discuss some of the problems we all have and get the opinions of you gentlemen as to what we can do about them. First I'd like to call on Bill Warner, state fish and game officer.'

Bill Warner was a trim, broad-shouldered man who looked like a college halfback. 'Already this winter I've found six instances of snowmobilers chasing deer and elk in deep snow.

'This is a really brutal thing. The animals get frantic with three or four machines howling along after them. They exhaust themselves trying to get away. Some of them are already weak from lack of browse – the deer in particular.

'After they quit running, the snowmobilers lose interest and go away, but some of those animals they've chased are too weak by then to recover. They die right there in the snow. I've found ten already this winter. One is too many.'

Sheriff Chip Briscoe, a heavyset, greying man with sharp dark eyes, was the next speaker.

'I flew over the lower end of this county last week,' he said. 'It seemed to me that every flat and every valley in it was crisscrossed with snowmobile tracks.

'There was a time when winter was a natural protection for remote summer homes, but now these cussed snow scooters can go anywhere. I've had seven complaints this winter about break-ins. Sometimes they stay two or three days, use up all the food in the cabins, then go on.

'But sometimes they steal everything they can haul away. I've solved one case out of the seven, and that was almost pure luck. I saw a snowmobile coming out of Squaw Creek one day, with a saddle on the hood. It happened to be two out-of-town sports. They'd raided Charley Bassham's summer home ten miles up Squaw Creek. We get a lot of out-of-town snowmobilers in here, but I'm not putting all the blame on them. We've got a few local crooks of our own.'

The sheriff stood for a moment, silent, scowling. 'Well, that's my complaint. And the county hasn't got a snowmobile to go chasing after these birds.'

Pete Bartholomew was the next speaker. 'Let me give you a few figures,' he began. 'Our summer count shows a hundred and seventeen thousand visitor days in this little district alone. Aside from the Big Ute ski area, we never used to even think of a winter count.

'But last year we made an estimate, at least. It showed about three thousand visitors in the Sawatch District from November to April. Now we think that estimate may have been a little low.' Pete shook his head.

Over in the corner, Lassie grunted as she shifted position in her sleep.

'The litter problem from those winter visitors gave us a bigger headache than all the summer people. There's a pattern to the way litter is scattered in summer – you know, along trails and roads, at picnic spots, around campgrounds. But in winter, because snowmobiles can go places where people can't even walk in summer, trash is thrown anywhere.' Pete waved his arms to indicate an explosion. 'We find plastic sacks twelve feet up in the branches of trees.

'In Crystal Basin – that's one of the favourite haunts of snowmobilers – we found the willows near Mirror Falls literally festooned with trash, willows that had been covered with snow a few months before. I don't think I've got all the trash out of Crystal Basin yet!'

Something bumped against the outside door. Lassie rose suddenly and crossed the room, and when Scott opened the door, there sat Chinook, panting and blowing vapour into the frosty air.

'I thought I sent him home when he started to follow me,' Pettigrew said.

The two dogs greeted each other amiably and Lassie went outside.

'I'm going to turn the safety part of the programme over to Tommy Thompson,' Pete said.

Thompson, the assistant ranger, was a lanky, freckle-faced man. He passed out printed sheets that detailed safety precautions for snowmobilers.

'I'd like to get these into the hands of every snowmobiler,' Thompson said. 'The radio station and the newspaper have both tried to help us out with stories and announcements. In November we had a meeting for all those interested in snowmobiling. There was good advance publicity on it.' Thompson grinned ruefully. 'Twenty people showed up.

'One thing that really bothers me is the way snowmobilers, and some skiers, too, completely disregard our warning signs near snowslide areas. I've seen snowmobiles pass within ten feet of the signs, and the drivers never even slowed up.'

Pettigrew nodded, studying the sheets. 'I've heard that engine noise and yelling don't start slides. Is that true?'

Thompson looked at Scott for the answer.

'No, it's not! Slides and avalanches can be triggered by noise or even a skier gliding silently across a slope.

'The signs are placed to warn everyone away from an area where slides usually run. A man on skis or snowshoes or on a machine is deliberately asking for it when he uses his own judgement about entering a posted avalanche area.'

Thompson referred again to the safety suggestions on the sheets. 'There's only one way we can ever hope to have these rules observed.' He paused. 'And that is if snowmobilers will take the responsibility of enforcement upon themselves.'

'Now you're getting down to the organisation of a club,' Benton said.

Thompson nodded. 'That's right.'

Pettigrew tapped his finger against the pages he was holding on his lap. 'These things are all good, yes. No one is going to argue against them. Never travel alone, always let someone know where you plan to go, wear the right clothing, have emergency food, tools, spare equipment, snowshoes – the whole list. Sure, it's all good!' Then he shook his head. 'But you simply can't order people to follow these rules and expect them to do it. They –'

'No one wants to *order* them, Mr Pettigrew,' Scott said. 'The Forest Service would very much prefer that snowmobilers, through organisations of their own, establish behaviour and safety codes and work among themselves to see that the rules are observed.'

'That sounds great,' Pettigrew said, 'but a lot of our snowmobilers wouldn't join a club if you paid them. Any time you try to organise a sport, all the fun goes out of it, and then all you've got is a bunch of hardheads arguing over byelaws and rules. Going to meetings becomes more important than the sport itself.'

'You're not against a club, are you?' Scott asked.

'Not at all!' Pettigrew insisted. 'I'd be the first to join, but out of the hundred and sixty-five people we've been talking about, I'll bet you wouldn't get more than thirty-five.'

Sheriff Briscoe stirred restlessly in his chair. 'I disagree with you, Pettigrew. Take the right approach, and I think you could get almost all the snowmobile nuts into a club.'

'Nuts, huh?' Pettigrew grinned. 'If you'd go out yourself on a Skimmer, instead of sending a deputy to investigate those break-in complaints, you'd be the biggest snowmobile nut of all.'

'I'd be a nut, all right, especially if I got bucked off into snow neck-deep about ten miles up Spar Creek in the middle of a blizzard.'

The men laughed. Jim Benton said, 'No worry, Sheriff. I'd send a Glory to get you out.'

The dogs were romping around outside. They banged against the storm door, and a moment later Scott heard Lassie bark from somewhere in the parking lot.

'What do you think about a snowmobile club, Mr Benton?' Scott asked.

Benton frowned. 'We did have a sort of club when there were only about fifteen snowmobiles in town, but it folded up from lack of interest. I'd say now that it would take at least three clubs.

'That way people of like interests could get together. Some like to race, some like just to cruise, a few like to camp out . . . There're all kinds of approaches to the sport. There are some people who are individuals. They wouldn't consider going out with a crowd any more than they would take fifteen or twenty people with them to go fishing.'

'Then you are in favour of clubs?' Scott asked.

'Yes, indeed. I've even tried to revive the informal group we used to have here, but it just didn't work out.' Benton spread his hands. 'It takes more than one man.'

'How many snowmobile dealers are there in town?' Scott asked.

'Six,' Thompson answered. 'I invited them all to this meeting, but four couldn't make it.'

Scott made a mental note to talk to those four dealers later. 'Snow sports are alike in some respects,' he said slowly. 'Take skiing, for example. When people get hurt because they disregard safety rules, and that includes having good equipment, it tends to scare others away from the sport. Now, skiing is often confined to a given area, where the operators and the ski patrol can exercise reasonable control. They can enforce safety precautions. Sure, there will be some injuries, because it's that kind of sport, but if someone busts a leg, say, he's going to be cared for quickly.

'Suppose a snowmobiler goes out alone and gets in a jam. He may freeze to death. One deal like that, and the sport will be called reckless and dangerous. It's a great sport. It doesn't deserve to get a bad name. I think dealers would be helped if they themselves worked to keep the sport safe. More people would be encouraged to buy snowmobiles.'

'Sure,' Pettigrew said. 'No argument about that.' He looked at Sheriff Briscoe. 'You mentioned the right approach to organising us nuts, Chip. What is the right approach?'

The sheriff leaned back in his chair. 'I haven't figured that out yet.'

They all looked at Scott then.

He, too, had to admit that he did not have the answer. 'I'm brand-new to the sport. In the next few weeks I expect to learn more about it and about the people in it, and then maybe I'll have some definite suggestions.'

I'd better have some good ideas, he told himself. He had been sent to the district to do a job, and it was up to him to get it done.

The meeting broke up a short time later. Everyone promised to cooperate in every way possible. Pete and Thompson and Scott looked at each other after the others had left.

'Well, the Forest Service still has the problem.' Thompson sighed in disappointment.

'We've got an idea planted, at least,' Pete said. 'That's a start. Now all Scott has to do is to stay with it and work it out.'

'Yeah.' Scott went to the door to let Lassie in. Her coat was shining from the cold. She sat down to lick ice from her paws.

Thompson grinned and said, 'How are you going to work it out, Scott?'

'To tell the truth, I'm not going to try. I'm going to join the Foreign Legion and forget the whole thing!'

'I've felt like that myself at times,' Pete laughed.

'By the way, do you have a phone in your room at Pine Haven?'

Scott nodded. 'It works only in the daytime. If you have any lost snowmobilers after six p.m., don't call me,' he added jokingly.

Pete was turning off the lights. 'I've heard of phones like that.'

Out in the cold night, Lassie lost no time in leaping into the green jeep when Scott opened the door. The district ranger and his assistant left in their cars, but Scott stood for a few moments longer looking at the dim bulk of the Menzies range west of town.

Tomorrow would be a good day to cruise into Crystal Basin. This time he would have all the emergency equipment that was on Thompson's list, and a shortwave radio, to boot.

The owner of the Pine Haven Motel, at the southern edge of Gateway, had no objection to dogs, and that was one reason Scott was staying there.

It seemed to him that he had barely got to sleep when the phone rang. He almost knocked the bedside light over before he got it turned on. He did knock the phone receiver to the floor while fumbling for it with his eyes closed, and then he drew it to him by the cord.

'Scott? This is Pete Bartholomew. I –'

'It's a lousy joke, Pete.' Scott opened one eye to look at his watch. It was 2.12 a.m. After listening for only a few moments, Scott spoke again. 'Aw, cut it out! Do you know what time it is?'

'I do, and I was just as sleepy as you a few minutes ago, but I'm not fooling.'

'You've got to be! A forest fire at this time of year, with the snow belly-deep on a tall Indian?'

'I'll meet you at the garage in fifteen minutes,' Pete said. He hung up.

Scott swung over to sit on the edge of the bed, shaking his head groggily. Lassie looked at him expectantly, stretching and yawning. At least *she* was ready to go, wherever it was.

Chapter 3

VIOLATORS

Pete Bartholomew rode with Scott on the way up Garnet Pass. Thompson was ahead of them in a jeep, pulling two Snow Rockets on a trailer, and ahead of Thompson was a pickup truck carrying three Forest Service employees.

'The state patrolman who spotted it about an hour ago radioed the sheriff's office, and they called me from there,' Pete explained. 'The patrolman said there had been snowmobiles in the Whale Creek area after dark, but he thinks they all came out of that area.'

Lassie was curled up on Scott's sleeping bag in the backseat, getting more sleep while she could.

'How do you start a forest fire in the winter?' Scott asked.

'We'll find out.'

A half hour later they reached the mouth of Whale Creek. They could see a faint glow about a mile south. 'That looks as if it's close to the old Tanner mine,' Pete said. 'Junipers below the cliffs, along the creek. I sure hope the wind doesn't come up.'

They drove off the highway to a state roadside park, and that was as far as they could go in the snow with the jeeps and the truck. The area was well chewed up with snowmobile tracks.

It took only a few minutes for the fire crew to get ready for the run up Whale Creek.

Pete was driving one snowmobile and Thompson the other, each with a man behind him. One man was on the sled behind Pete and that left the other trailer for Scott.

It was already pretty well loaded with tools, so Scott said, 'I'll walk in. I need a good workout on snowshoes, anyway.'

He left the jeep door tied open so Lassie could get in and out, and then he put on his webs and started after the snowmobiles. So many machines had been up and down the road that Scott found the going easy at first.

Sitting beside the jeep, Lassie seemed to think that she could have made it, too, for she barked for permission to follow, but Scott called, 'No deal, Lassie. Stay!'

Before long he was walking past red cliffs that rose above a narrow gulch, where junipers grew thickly beside a frozen creek. In the shadows of the trees, the snow was deep and coarse and shifting under his webs, unpacked even by the passage of many snowmobiles.

Standing in the cold starlight above the cliffs were dense thickets of spruce trees. Scott knew then why Pete had worried about the wind. A fire down here by the creek, if driven by strong gusts, could throw embers to ignite the trees above the cliffs, setting off a chain of fires.

He came upon the fire fighters where the gulch had widened into a little cove near some old mine buildings. Wisps of smoke were still rising from the charred skeletons of the juniper trees, but the fire had been contained.

There were snowmobile tracks all over the area.

'Take a look,' Pete said, and he showed Scott where the fire had started.

Not far from a huge juniper, someone had kicked the snow away and built a big bonfire. It was still steaming a little under the snow the crew had shovelled over it.

'They didn't think it would spread,' Pete explained, 'but it was big enough to dry out the needle mat and eat its way over to the tree. Once those dead twigs at the bottom of the tree got going – well, you can see how close together the junipers are.'

'Were,' Scott said. He looked around at the burned-out cove. It had been a beautiful little spot. Trees to replace those killed by the fire would not have time to grow during his lifetime. It angered him to think that the fire had been caused by sheer carelessness. It would not have taken three minutes for one of the snowmobilers to kick snow on to the bonfire.

'One thing – ' Pete looked around – 'they don't appear to have left any litter.'

'This was a good bunch,' Scott said. 'They don't throw their trash around. They just start forest fires.'

It was daylight when they left the cove by the old Tanner mine. By then there was not a wisp of smoke or a spark or a plume of steam left anywhere.

The trampled snow, stained with charred fragments, and the stark skeletons of the dead trees made an ugly picture in the full light.

They loaded up and started back to town. Scott rode out on the trailer behind Thompson. They had gone only about a mile when they saw Bill Warner, the state fish and game officer, unloading a snowmobile beside the road. The pickup went on, but Scott and Pete and Thompson stopped to talk to the warden.

'Fire all out?' Warner asked.

'Yep,' Pete said. 'What are you up to?'

Warner got a half-gallon thermos of coffee from his pickup. 'Interested in a shot of this?'

'Man, you're talking!' Thompson said.

As they drank the hot coffee, Warner kept looking at the rolling hills and timbered ridges south of the highway. 'No tracks showing from here, but that same patrolman who spotted the fire heard rifle shots off that way about dusk last night, when he was giving a ticket to a guy.'

'That's elk country over there,' Pete mused.

'Yeah.' Warner looked at Scott. 'Want to learn a little more about snowmobiling?'

'You've got a customer,' Scott said. 'Pete, will you take Lassie back to –'

'Bring her along,' Warner cut in. 'I'm taking the sled. I've got a radio, and if we get stuck, we can get help from Emerald Lake pretty fast.'

Warner's machine was a Wilderness King. It was a workhorse for power, and Warner was an experienced driver. With Lassie smugly surveying the snowy country from her dry seat on a plastic tarpaulin and other gear in the trailer, they went about two miles over unbroken snow before Warner stopped.

Because of engine noise, conversation between the two men on the snowmobile was difficult. A few times Scott leaned forward to shout a question into Warner's ear, but he soon gave that up.

Just under the crest of a wind-scoured ridge, Warner parked. The snow was so thin that there was no way to cross without scraping rocks. They walked on up to the top. Lassie jumped out of the trailer and went exploring among the rocks.

'If there's anyone over in there now, they'd be about where you see those aspen thickets,' Warner said. 'The wind keeps some of those sidehills fairly clear, and it's great grass country. At this time of year there's always an elk herd in there.'

They went around the ridge. The sun was out in full force now, and both men were wearing snow goggles.

Though they saw no snowmobile tracks, Warner seemed to know exactly where he was going.

He stopped on top of a hill. 'There they are.'

They were looking down at a small, weathered cabin at the edge of a little park. Two snowmobiles were parked beside the cabin, and three men were standing in front of it. Obviously they had heard the visitors coming.

'Brad Parris in the tan jacket,' Warner said. 'That's Oscar Renfrow in the blue parka. I can't make out that other fellow.'

'Game poachers?'

'I've never yet nailed them, let's say.'

'Is that private ground?' Scott asked.

'Nope! National forest. That's an old line camp from the days when the Circle T ran five thousand head of cattle. Hunters have kept fixing it up a little every year. I wish you Forest Service guys would burn it down.'

Open to the sun, the snow in the little park was fairly well settled. It was so tracked up that Scott thought the three men must have been racing their machines around and across it.

'Hiya, Warden!' Brad Parris yelled as Warner drove up. 'What brings you out in the heat of the day?' He was a burly, fair-skinned man, with a wide grin. He was all good nature, it seemed, and completely unalarmed by Warner's visit.

'Just touring for our health,' Warner said evenly. 'How about you fellows?'

'Same thing,' Parris said jovially.

Oscar Renfrow, the man in the blue parka, showed white teeth against a black beard stubble as he grinned and invited Warner and Scott into the cabin for a cup of coffee.

The third man was younger than the other two. He sat on a chopping block in the cleared space before the cabin and merely watched. When Lassie sniffed inquiringly at his pants legs, he pushed her away.

'Come on in and have some coffee,' Parris insisted.

'No, thanks,' Warner said. 'Seen any elk on your travels around?'

'Seven yesterday, when we were coming in by Hecla Mountain. Nice-looking bull in the bunch.' Parris watched Lassie trot out on the packed snow, where the machines had made a firm surface.

With her long hair flying, she raced down the track for the sheer joy of the exercise.

'Sure you won't have some coffee?' Renfrow said.

Warner grinned. 'All right! Since you boys are so determined to show me that you don't have any illegal meat in there, let's go.'

The man on the chopping block stayed where he was. He seemed to have no interest in anything but sitting and watching the hills.

The interior of the cabin was hot and stuffy from the fire in a small cookstove, and the one small window did not admit much light. Renfrow did not help illumination by standing in the doorway.

After his eyes became adjusted to the gloom, Scott

looked the room over carefully. There was scarcely any likely hiding place for part of an elk in the small interior.

Sitting on campstools, Scott and Warner drank the coffee Parris poured into plastic cups. 'You've got a pretty snug little camp,' Warner said.

'We like it.' Parris shrugged. 'It's a good place when you just want to get away from town for a few days. You know?'

'Yeah, I know.'

Parris grinned. 'You've got a suspicious mind, Warden. Want to search the sleeping bags?'

Warner smiled and shook his head. He glanced at Renfrow, who was still blocking the doorway. 'You boys came in by Hecla Mountain, huh?'

'Yep,' Parris said.

'Going out the same way?'

'That's hard to say.'

Warner nodded. He sipped his coffee. 'What range do you get out of that little transmitter in the sleeping bag over there?'

Scott had not noticed the radio. It took him a few moments to spot the top of it showing in the rolls of a sleeping bag.

'It doesn't reach too far,' Parris said. 'Maybe a mile, if conditions are right.' He glanced quickly at Renfrow.

'Well, thanks for the coffee,' Warner said, rising. 'I guess we'll get along now.'

The moment Scott stepped outside, the reflection of sun from the snow smashed into his eyes and he pulled his goggles down.

Lassie was still out in the little park, on one of the beaten snowmobile trails. She was not running now.

She was digging in the snow. Then she looked towards Scott and barked.

'What do you know?' Warner said. 'I think she's found something out there.'

Lassie had indeed smelled out something, for she went back to digging and then dragged a dark brown object to the surface.

'From here that looks like meat,' Warner said. 'I'm willing to bet it's elk.'

Scott studied the faces of the three campers.

Only the man on the chopping block looked nervous and scared. Parris and Renfrow were still cool customers.

'Would you say that was elk meat, Parris?' Warner asked.

'I haven't the least idea. Even if it is, a lot of snowmobiles have been through that park. There were tracks before we got here.' A lot of Parris's good nature had vanished. His face was now hard and wary.

Still, he was able to grin. 'If you've got any idea of tying us to that – whatever it is out there – forget it, Warden. It isn't in our possession. Anyone could have put it there.'

From a legal standpoint, he was completely right, Scott thought. Rather simple and clever, burying the meat in the snow and then running over the hiding place repeatedly with the machines.

And there was the radio, too. Scott was willing to bet that it would transmit much farther than a mile. When the poachers were ready to go out with their illegal game, they could contact friends waiting at any one of a dozen approaches to the area and make sure that the coast was clear.

There just did not seem to be a case that would stand up in court.

Warner casually put his hand on the shoulder of the man sitting on the chopping block. The next instant he dragged the man off the block and sent him sprawling on his stomach.

The surface of the block was stained with dried blood, and there were bits of bone in the crevices of the axe marks. With the point of a knife, Warner scraped and dug, putting the evidence in a little plastic bag. 'The laboratory technicians can tell us something about this.'

For the first time Parris was angry. 'What will that prove? Somebody chopped meat up on that block. That's all you can prove!'

'You were pretty anxious to keep the block covered,' Warner said.

'Willie had a right to sit there!' Parris shouted. 'I think you'd better get out of here – and take your snoopy dog with you!'

'We'll do that in a few minutes, and you three are going along. You're under arrest for illegal possession of elk meat. Now, I'll explain your rights to you . . .'

The explanation took only a short time, and then Warner said to Scott, 'Call Lassie in, will you?'

While Lassie was racing back at Scott's command, Warner went into the cabin and returned with a frying pan. 'You should have washed this, Parris. Don't you know the odour of fried elk liver hangs on forever?'

'That's private property you're stealing!' Parris raged. 'You've got no right to –'

'It's evidence,' Warner said calmly, 'so shut up.' He showed the pan to Scott. 'See how the grease congealed around a couple of pieces they didn't eat and left in the pan?'

Warner had seen plenty when he went into the cabin, Scott thought. He himself had noticed the pan on the floor behind the stove, but he had not observed as keenly as Warner.

'They threw out a couple of pieces,' Warner said. 'Since Lassie has a pretty good nose . . .'

Lassie got the idea after Warner let her sniff the pan and after Scott directed her to several logical places where the strips of liver might have been thrown.

She found the meat, where it had been tossed into the snow and crushed down with a boot.

Parris exploded, then, in a tirade against Willie. 'I told you to burn that liver, you idiot! All you had to do was dump it in the stove, but you –'

'Old bigmouth!' Willie yelled. 'All you do is give orders. "Willie, do the dishes! Willie, chop some wood!" Your big fat idea of burying that elk meat wasn't so smart, was it?'

'If it hadn't been for that nosy dog . . .' Renfrow cast a dark look at Lassie.

'All right, all right!' Parris growled. 'So we killed an elk and got caught. We're not going to hang for it, so everybody stop yelling and get packing.'

He glared at Warner. 'But if you think we're going to help you haul the meat in –'

'It'll be hauled in, don't you worry.' Warner had stowed the fried liver in the plastic bag and put the frying pan in the tool box of his snowmobile.

Now the warden ran up the antenna of his radio and began to talk to fish and game officers at Emerald Lake, ten miles away. After that he went out to examine the piece of meat Lassie had found under the snowmobile tracks in the park.

He reburied it.

Going back to the highway, Warner drove behind the machines of the poachers. Scott found himself yawning. In one day he had been given a close look at two serious problems created by snowmobiles, and that was only a beginning.

The problems would unfold easily enough, he was sure. It was the answers to them that would be the challenge.

He hoped his next lesson would start at a better hour than two o'clock in the morning.

Chapter 4

CRYSTAL BASIN

Much to her disgust, Lassie had to stay with Pete during the first two trips Scott took deep into the mountains.

One afternoon in the district ranger's office, Pete said, 'She isn't very happy doing office work, Scott. Why don't you take her along on your trip into Crystal Basin tomorrow?'

'Way back there in that deep snow? If anything went wrong, I could come out on snowshoes, but I'd have to carry her.'

Lassie was watching and listening as if she understood what the two men were saying.

'You've got all the equipment for survival, and you've got a radio. Let's say the Rocket conks out or you get stuck.' Pete waved one hand. 'So what's the big problem?'

'You're saying that the worst that could happen to me is spending a night out in the snow.'

'Maybe not even that. If there were any real emergency involved, we could get you out even at night.'

Scott thought it over. 'All right, Lassie. You can go along tomorrow.'

Lassie was ready to start right then. She whined and headed for the door.

Scott spent the rest of the afternoon talking to snowmobile dealers. He and Pete and Thompson had agreed that it would be wise to keep the idea of forming clubs simmering along, but not to push so strongly that the snowmobilers would think they were being ordered around.

Thompson was doing some groundwork, too, and, as soon as it seemed that the club idea had taken hold, he planned to call another public meeting.

In the evening Scott went to the courthouse to visit Sheriff Briscoe.

'I hear you've been getting around some in snowmobile country,' the sheriff said.

'A little. I'm going into Crystal Basin tomorrow.'

'Fine! Now, I know this isn't your job, but I would appreciate it if you'd sort of check the summer homes at Wildcat Falls when you go by. You know, just look 'em over to see if everything seems all right.'

'Sure.'

The sheriff leaned back in his chair. 'Maybe you don't know it, but you sort of put a kink in your rope when you helped Warner catch those game violators.'

'How's that?'

'Their trial was this afternoon. They got off pretty easy, considering. Two-hundred-dollar fine apiece. The thing of it is that, aside from the snowmobile dealers, Brad Parris is the one man who could have done more than anyone I know to help get a club organised.'

That surprised Scott. 'Brad Parris?'

'Yeah, him.' The sheriff nodded. 'He owns a big feedlot west of town. Makes a pile of money. He's got the reputation of being about the best snowmobiler in the country. Last winter he promoted a tour across the Menzies to Larb City and back. A hundred and twenty machines and about two hundred people from half a dozen states. He's a real good organiser.'

And a game poacher, Scott thought. It did indeed seem that Parris would have been a valuable man to help get snowmobilers to police their own sport, but now he was undoubtedly nursing a grudge against Scott and Lassie.

It was a bad break, all right, but even if Scott had known all about Parris before the arrests at the old Circle T line camp, it would not have made any difference in his doing what he had done to help Warner.

'Give him a chance to cool off,' the sheriff advised. 'Brad isn't a bad guy. I'll talk to him later, and maybe we can still get some help from him.'

It seemed doubtful to Scott, but he nodded.

The sun was just knocking the frosty bite out of the air the next morning when he unloaded the Rocket and sled six miles below Wildcat Falls. He checked all his gear carefully, while Lassie kept crowding against him, anxious to get in the sled trailer.

He was close to the immense thrusts of two snowy peaks between which the Crystal Basin road ran. The road itself was fairly well packed from snowmobile travel, but on both sides of it, in the aspen thickets, the snow was unbroken.

It was fenced, private land down here, but in winter it was still a wilderness. Scott reacted to it with the sheer joy of looking, and twice he ran out of the beaten track into soft snow.

The second time he did it, with Lassie's sled lurching and tipping a little as he climbed back into the broken trail, Lassie barked sharp disapproval at his carelessness.

'Watch that stuff!' she seemed to say.

There were six summer homes below Wildcat Falls, some of them huge, expensive structures. Scott cruised slowly around them, looking at windows and doors for signs of forced entrance. Everything seemed to be all right.

A half mile farther on, the peaks pinched in against the stream and the road. Scott found himself climbing steeply, getting higher and higher above the creek in a canyon.

Pete had warned him about a place the snowmobilers called Heartthrob Point, but Scott did not recognise it until too late.

For about three feet, the outer edge of the rocky road was exposed because the wind had blown the snow away, but from the inner edge of the bare strip to the high-cut bank, the drifts lay at a steep slant.

It seemed to Scott that the snowmobilers who had gone before him might have hugged the bank a little more, but the slanting track was very close to the bare strip of road.

When suddenly he hit Heartthrob Point, he was on rippled ice that slanted towards the canyon on his left. He gunned the Rocket and steered towards the bank, but the machine slid towards the outside edge.

There was one desperate instant when he was looking almost straight down at the tops of trees along Crystal Creek, a hundred feet below. The Rocket was tilted, and his left elbow was hanging in space.

Fortunately it was a narrow tongue of ice that spring flow from the bank had laid across the road. The crawler track kept digging. All at once Scott was beyond the ice, back in the snowy track.

He stopped and looked around. Lassie was gone. The sled was there, but she must have been thrown out and over the bank when it tilted.

'Oh, no!' Scott leaped up to go back.

And then he saw Lassie. She had not been thrown over the bank. Even before the trailer struck the ice, she had jumped, and she was just now struggling out of a snowbank on the high side of the road.

She sniffed at the treacherous ice, and then she scurried across it to Scott and shook herself vigorously to throw off the snow.

'I would have jumped, too, if I could have!' Scott laughed.

He looked back at the ice. He could see now that a thin layer of snow had blown over the rippled surface, making it difficult to tell at a glance what lay beneath.

He would not forget the place. It had been well named.

Before long they were out of the canyon, and the view ahead began to widen. Through occasional breaks in the tall, quiet spruce and fir trees, Scott caught glimpses of a towering semicircle of snowy mountains at the upper end of the basin.

He passed old mines with sagging buildings and a huge ore mill that was slowly tumbling off its steep slope.

When he broke out of the timber to where he had a fairly open view of the basin, he stopped for a while to look at the winter wilderness in its full, rugged beauty.

There were no fresh tracks in the road – a road that lay twelve feet or more above the surface of the ground. A snowmobile, he thought, was truly a remarkable machine.

He went on and on. As the basin widened, he saw old tracks of snowmobiles diverging from the main route in dozens of places. From his study of a map, he knew where he was going.

Scott kept the sturdy Rocket climbing until he was not far below timberline at the end of the road on the dump of the McKimson mine. The whole basin lay before him.

He saw five frozen lakes, patches of dark timber, beaver ponds on the benches where streams lay beneath the snow. Wind was whipping snow pennants high on the mountains, though it was almost windless where Scott was.

For a while he had a feeling that the whole scene was his alone, that he was the only man who had ever seen this great basin that had been gouged out by a glacier in ancient times.

There was room in a place like this for hundreds of people to roam without crowding each other. Anyone who wanted to had the right to be there, summer or winter.

They owned Crystal Basin, all the people of the United States. It was theirs to enjoy. And, at the same time, it was theirs to respect. To shut off such a place from winter use was unthinkable. To allow it to be filled with trash was also unthinkable!

Scott was drinking coffee when he heard the distant humming sounds. Lassie was exploring the edges of the ruined buildings, where wind had whirled the snow away. She put her front paws on the crusted top of a snowbank and stood up to peer into the basin.

'Sounds like a whole herd of snowmobiles, huh, Lassie? After a while we'll go down and see.'

Later, shortcutting through the timber in the

general direction of Blue Lake, Scott came out on a bench and saw at least twenty snowmobiles below him.

About half of them were racing on the frozen surface of the lake, making tight turns, skidding, sometimes nearly flipping. For a while he could not make any sense or pattern out of their antics. It looked like bedlam and sounded the same way.

Then he puzzled it out. Two teams of five machines each were running side by side on slalom courses on the frozen surface. The snowmobilers had put down coats and jackets to mark the gates.

They were having a great time, yelling, charging into the gates, going full tilt. Scott saw one driver fall off his machine and slide for fifteen feet. The other contestants and the spectators whooped with laughter.

Scott had to backtrack to find a way down. By the time he got to the lake, the racing was over. Some of the snowmobilers were out on the ice, but most of them were standing around their machines or near a fire, where coffee was brewing.

Those close to where Scott stopped his machine welcomed him with friendly greetings, but he observed a slight cooling in their attitude when a man in a knit cap with a long tassel asked, 'Aren't you the Forest Service guy who's going to clamp down on snowmobiles?'

'Where'd you get that idea?'

The man introduced himself and the tall blond girl with him – Jerry Wayne and Barbara Vogel. 'That's the story that's been going around,' Wayne replied. 'We even heard that the Forest Service was going to close this basin to snowmobiling.'

'Not as far as I know,' Scott said. 'Why should the area be restricted?'

Wayne shrugged. 'We don't know of any reason, but that's the rumour.'

'This is the first I've heard of it.' Keeping the public accurately informed about Forest Service plans and policies was always a chore, Scott thought. Too many people preferred to believe stories out of thin air rather than to take two minutes to call someone like Pete Bartholomew and get the truth.

Following his plan of getting to know as many snowmobilers as possible, Scott circulated among the group. The area had been used so frequently by machines that it was well packed. Lassie had no trouble getting around, as long as she stayed out of the soft snow.

This was a young group, Scott observed. Some of them, he found out, were college students home on vacation, but most of them were married couples from Gateway.

He talked for a while to the Hunters, who said they had taken up snowmobiling only recently. 'We've never had so much fun in all our lives,' Joe Hunter said.

'Is this a club you people have?' Scott asked.

'Not really.' Lucille Hunter shook her head. 'We don't have a name or any rules to speak of. We just get together at times for trips like this.'

'About the only regulation we have is keeping the places we go clean,' Hunter added. 'Whatever we haul in, we haul out – except for the food, of course.'

Scott was happy to hear that. 'Who's responsible for the idea?'

'The Forest Service suggested it,' Hunter said. 'Tommy Thompson, I think it was, two winters ago, but Jerry Wayne really started hammering at the idea this winter.

'You see, Wayne was about the first man in here last spring with his jeep. He said he saw trash hanging around everywhere like crêpe paper after a high-school football game, so he started promoting the keep-it-clean idea.'

Good for him, Scott thought. 'He's a sort of organiser, huh?'

Mrs Hunter nodded. 'Jerry figures out the trips, calls people, and keeps things going.'

Here could be a key man – just the sort of fellow who could do a lot to reduce the problems caused by snowmobiling. Scott made a mental note to have a talk with Jerry Wayne later.

Except for a couple of diehards out on the lake, the group began to eat lunch about the same time. Scott got out his sandwiches and sat on his machine, talking to the Morrals, whose red Malemute was parked next to his Rocket.

Jeff Morral was a Gateway attorney. Sandy, his wife, was a good-looking woman in blue stretch pants.

'Ice can be pretty tricky and dangerous,' Scott said, watching the two men on the lake. A large part of the surface had been blown clear of snow by the wind, but reaching out from the banks were sharp-spined drifts four or five feet high. The two snowmobilers were vying with each other by trying to plough through the drifts at full speed. 'Have you looked that ice over carefully?' Scott asked.

'Jerry Wayne did,' Morral said. 'He drilled holes to determine the thickness, scouted around for thin places – I know he checked pretty thoroughly.'

'Can I give Lassie part of my lunch?' Mrs Morral asked.

'She's been trained not to accept handouts.'

'That's good!' The woman patted Lassie's head.

A moment later Scott poured the rest of his coffee, about half a cup.

'There's plenty over at the fire,' Morral said.

The fire had been puzzling Scott for some time. It was going strongly in a hollow in the snow, yet he could tell that it was not down on the surface of the ground.

Wayne and Barbara Vogel and four others were standing close to it when Scott walked over with his cup.

Then it struck him.

The fire was on top of a concrete table. This was a Forest Service campground. Because of the snow, it had been easy to reach dead limbs on the trees nearby.

Wayne put on gloves and lifted the coffeepot, ready to fill Scott's cup, but Scott was no longer interested in coffee.

He could see enough of the tabletop to know that it was ruined. The heat had disintegrated the concrete and cracked it. 'Who built that fire on the table?'

Wayne put the coffeepot down slowly. No one said anything.

Wanton destruction of campground facilities, placed at great expense for the benefit and use of thousands of people, always enraged Scott, but he had learned over the years to control his temper.

He waited for an answer to his question.

It seemed that no one was going to speak, but then Barbara Vogel said, 'Jerry?'

He gave her a quick, angry look. 'I built it! I didn't realise the concrete was going to come apart like dried mud.'

'No concrete can stand that heat,' Scott said.

'All right, I did it, not thinking!' Wayne snapped. 'Now what do you want from me?'

'You could stop shouting,' Barbara suggested.

'Stay out of this!' Wayne told her.

'Don't you yell at me, Jerry Wayne!'

Wayne looked at Scott. 'You and I can settle our problem later, if you don't mind. Okay?' He was angry clear through, and it was hard to tell in how many directions his anger extended.

Scott nodded.

'Come on, Barbara.' Wayne took the girl's arm and they walked down towards the lake. They stood there arguing.

Now the group at the fire, while not hostile towards Scott, were definitely cool in their attitude. 'You want us to put it out?' a man asked.

'No. Let it go now.' Scott went back to the Morrals.

'What do you do now?' Morral asked. 'Take us all before a United States commissioner? We're all guilty. I saw Wayne building the fire, but I didn't know it would wreck the table.'

'You and your legal mind, Jeff,' said Sandy. 'We'll all pay for the table, that's what!' She looked towards the lake. 'And this isn't the first time Jerry and Barbara have been in a fight. He would have admitted he built the fire, if she had just given him a little more time.'

'I hate to agree with my wife,' Morral said, 'but she's right. Jerry was madder at himself than at you, because he realised he'd done a stupid thing. If Barbara had kept still, he might have cooled off, but you know women . . .' He grinned at Scott.

'Oh, be quiet, Jeff,' Sandy said. 'Here, Scott, have some of my coffee.'

Down at the lake, the argument seemed to be getting more heated. Suddenly, with an angry gesture,

Barabara turned away from Wayne and walked out on the ice.

Things just were not breaking right, Scott thought. For the second time, through no fault of his own, he had got crosswise with someone who could have been a big help to him.

'I've got a pretty good idea of why the Forest Service sent you into this district,' Morral said. He paused. 'It isn't going very well, is it?'

'Terribly. About the next thing that's going to happen is Lassie's biting me.'

Chapter 5

THE SNOW DUST TWINS

They were racing in teams of three on the lake after lunch. The engines made so much noise that Scott did not hear the new arrivals at the campground until they were almost there.

They were the Pettigrew boys, on their blue Skimmers, with Chinook riding behind Ted.

Lassie trotted over to greet Chinook. Before long the two dogs were frisking in the snow.

'Hey, Scott!' Bob shouted. 'How are you doing today?'

'Fine.'

'You raced yet?' Ted asked.

'No, and that's only half of it.'

'Aw, come on!' Ted urged. 'You and me and Bob can team up. We'll show 'em something, huh?'

'Just a minute!' Scott laughed. 'I followed you two one time, remember? And I got into a mess.'

'No tricks,' Bob said. 'We promise. We'll put you in the middle. That way you can see how I make the turns on the ice, and –'

'No, thanks. In a few minutes I'm going to tour around the basin.'

Barbara came up to them. 'Well! The Snow Dust

Twins. We wondered how long it would take you two to show up.'

Snow Dust Twins – that amused Scott. It was a good name for the boys. Barbara's next words caught Scott by surprise.

'Can I ride back with you?' she asked.

Scott hesitated. 'I'm not going down right away. I'm going to look the basin over.'

'That's all right. The others aren't going back very soon, either. I'll wait here, and you can pick me up when you're ready.'

'What's the matter with old Jerry?' Ted asked. 'You and him get into another –'

Scott shook his head at the boy. The last thing he needed was to make the breach between him and Jerry Wayne wider by hauling his girl back to town.

'Can I ride with you?' Barbara asked again.

'You didn't get things patched up?'

The girl shook her head. 'There's two people to all the other machines, or I wouldn't bother you.' She waited for an answer.

'I guess me or Bob could haul you back,' Ted said.

'No, thanks, Ted. I've seen you and Bob shoot across the ice at Heartthrob. I don't need that kind of thrill.'

'All right,' Scott said. He could not very well get out of it. 'If you change your mind about going with Jerry –'

'I won't,' Barbara said flatly. 'I'll be here.'

Scott saw Jerry Wayne watching them from the edge of the lake. Maybe Barbara would change her mind about going back with Jerry, despite what she had just said.

'Let's take a tour with Scott,' Ted said to his

brother. 'We can show him anything he wants to see in the basin.'

'Yeah!' Bob agreed.

Whether he liked it or not, Scott had Barbara to haul back to town, and now he also had the Snow Dust Twins as escorts.

'This time, you guys follow me,' he said.

Lassie came running to get in the trailer as soon as Scott started the engine. Chinook leaped on the seat behind Ted with such haste that he shot across the narrow surface and fell off on the other side.

Ted pushed the husky away when he started to get back on. 'You can run for a while.'

Scott took the road back towards the McKimson mine, with the two Skimmers crowding hard behind him. Chinook brought up the rear, plunging along the track with a speed that amazed Scott.

After half a mile, Scott turned off on the road that led down to the campground at Looking Glass Lake. Snowmobiles had broken a trail sometime before, but now it was blown over with fluffy snow.

The Rocket sent clouds of fine snow pluming into the air as it churned through – snow dust. Behind Scott the Snow Dust Twins yelled for more speed.

Scott found himself going a little faster for the sheer fun of it.

He stopped at Looking Glass Lake. There was a campground here somewhere, he knew, but now the tables and fire stands and even the signs were buried.

There had been plenty of snowmobiles in the area, but there was no evidence that anyone had dug down to one of the tables and built a fire on top of it.

'You worried about your old tables?' Ted asked.

'They're your tables as much as mine. Yes, I'm concerned about them. Aren't you?'

Ted knocked snow from his dark Cossack hat by beating it against the hood of the Skimmer. He frowned. 'I guess I never thought much about it. Those are wooden tables down there.' He jabbed his finger towards the snow.

Chinook, who had stayed right with them and was not even breathing hard from the run, got off the beaten track and fell almost out of sight. Safe in her trailer, Lassie barked encouragement to him.

He did not need it. The way Chinook could handle himself in deep snow was enough to make Scott shake his head.

'Old Jerry wasn't the first guy to build a fire on that table at Blue Lake,' Bob said. 'Somebody got that idea before the snow was higher than the tables, and then everybody else just did it.'

'Was it the right thing to do?' Scott asked.

'I guess not,' Bob said. 'So what are you going to do? Throw everybody in jail?'

'No. What do you suggest ought to be done?'

Bob's answer was not what Scott expected. 'What you ought to do is build a big platform out of iron, so it would stick up as high as the snow in winter. Then people could build a fire on it, and it wouldn't hurt a thing.'

Scott stared at the boy quietly. 'Where'd you get that idea, Bob?'

'I don't know. It just sort of came to me, I guess.'

'You may have something.'

Ted was growing restless. 'Are we going to sit here all day? I thought you wanted to see the basin, Scott.'

It was a perfect day for snowmobiling. The wind was light, and the sun was warm. Across a long bench of sparkling snow, they followed a track towards the

Deep Lake campground, the highest one in Crystal Basin.

They drove below a ridge, where a cornice of snow was hanging in a great curve. Though he could see part of the trail ahead, where snowmobiles had gone past the ridge, Scott stopped.

'What's the matter?' Ted yelled.

Scott pointed up at the cornice. 'That could come down and trigger a snowslide just about the time we're crossing below it.'

'Aw, we've been through there a lot of times!' Ted scoffed. 'Nothing happened.'

'One time is all it takes.' Scott took the radio out of its protective case on the rack on the outside of the backrest. In a few moments he was talking to Pete Bartholomew.

Scott told where he was and described the ridge. 'Has this area been posted with avalanche signs?'

'Not yet. It's on the list for next summer. It ran at least twice last winter. If you go over to the edge of the bench, you can see how it cleaned out the alpine firs below.'

Scott put the radio away. He made a wide turn and started back the way they had come. The boys followed.

They toured the Sugar Bowl, a big hollow with gently sloping sides. It was more like a saucer than a bowl, Scott thought.

The Snow Dust Twins took out ahead of him and raced around the saucer-like bowl, kneeling on the seat. Still untired, Chinook sat down by Lassie's sled and waited for the boys to make the circle.

Later, going towards Feather Falls through unbroken snow, Chinook got on behind Ted.

For fifty feet the water came down a dark face of

granite in short cascades. The rocks were glittering with ice, and the sound of the water was muted.

'Boy! Think of all the people who never get a chance to see anything like that!' Bob said.

'Huh!' Ted said. 'It's just a doggone old frozen waterfall. Let's go. I've seen this place a million times.'

They were below Blue Lake then, and near the southern edge of the basin. Leaving Feather Falls, the twins got ahead of Scott. Ted led them across a snowbridge over a branch stream.

Scott was on it before he realised where he was going. He looked down fifteen feet and saw a dark spot of moving water. When he got to the other side, he stopped and shouted until the boys looked back and throttled to a standstill.

'Don't you ever go across a place like that again, Ted!'

'It scared me, too,' Bob said. 'Those things can give in pretty easy.'

Scott realised that it was getting late when he heard the snowmobiles going down the basin road. From where he and the Snow Dust Twins were, they could not see the machines, but there was no doubt that they were leaving.

Scott was back in the lead. He headed for Blue Lake.

Barbara was waiting at the campground.

Never bashful about speaking his mind, Ted said, 'You're sure going to make old Jerry mad by swiping his girl, Scott.'

'Shall we leave her here?'

'No,' Ted answered, 'but you're sure going to make old Jerry sore.'

'I heard you the first time.' Scott unlashed his snowshoes. With Barbara helping, he threw snow on the fire, using the webs as shovels.

Afterwards he looked ruefully at the cracked, ruined table. He would tell the district ranger about it, and then it would be up to him to take whatever action he chose.

The sun was gone, and the air was getting crisp. In another hour it would be plenty cold in the basin.

'I'm not racing you two out of here,' Scott told the Snow Dust Twins. 'If you want to go ahead – '

'We'll follow you,' Ted interrupted. 'I want to see Barbara jump off just before Heartthrob Point.'

'Lassie jumped off on the way up, when she saw me skidding towards the canyon.'

Barbara laughed. 'You're saying that I'm at least as smart as Lassie.'

'How do you boys take that ice?' Scott asked.

'Like idiots,' Barbara said. 'I've seen them.'

'The first two times we went over it, we stopped and dug some dirt and old leaves and stuff out of the bank,' Bob said. 'When you scatter stuff like that on the ice, it helps.'

'That's the chicken way to cross,' Ted said. 'You won't to go into the canyon if you give it the gas and then charge,' he added.

Going downhill, Scott found the track fast. The increasing cold was making it all the better. In a short time they were at the Klondike mill. While Scott was getting a plastic bag out of the toolbox, Chinook and Lassie began to root around for rats in the dark, sagging structure.

Scott filled the sack with fine dirt he found under some huge leaning timbers of the mill. He looked at Ted. 'I'm one of the chickens you were talking about.'

Lassie remembered the Point. Both she and Barbara chose not to ride across it, even after Scott had scattered the fine dirt on the ice.

In spite of the dirt, Scott's machine slid sidewise, but it was not as bad as before, and it did not take him by surprise. He pulled on down the road far enough to give the boys room.

The Snow Dust Twins took a run at the ice and drove across like wild men. Scott had to admit that they did not skid as much as he had, but their method was still not the best way to handle a dangerous tongue of ice.

Passing the cabins below Wildcat Falls, Scott glanced over at them and kept going. They seemed to be as secure as when he had checked them a few hours before.

Then Ted, who was driving immediately behind Scott, honked his horn three times. He pulled up beside Scott when the latter stopped.

'I saw something move at one of those little upstairs windows in that chalet over there,' Ted said.

It was dusk. There was a great quietness on the snowy scene.

'I saw something move,' Ted repeated.

'Maybe the owner – '

'No! ' Ted shook his head. 'They live in Oklahoma. They never come up here after the hunting season.'

'Stay here with the boys,' Scott told Barbara.

She obeyed, and the boys stayed on the road, but Chinook came plopping through the snow after Scott when he drove over to the chalet.

There were no tracks in front of the building.

On the side away from the road there was a wide porch. The snow was almost level with it. Someone had driven a snowmobile on to the porch, but there was no sign of the machine from where Scott sat.

He hesitated for a moment. This was law enforcement business he was getting into, if someone was inside the building. Still, it was part of the whole problem of snowmobiling; and he had promised the sheriff to check out the cabins.

Chinook had no qualms about the matter. He thumped up on to the porch and went to the door. He put one paw against it, and it opened readily.

Scott quickly got his radio out of the pack. 'Stay, Lassie!'

It was a wide door. Scott felt the heat coming through it as soon as he was close. He peered around the casing and saw a snowmobile inside, a White Charger. The tiled floor around it was wet from melted snow.

Chinook was thumping around in another room as if he owned the place.

'Hello!' Scott called.

There was no answer.

His eyes were now getting adjusted to the dim interior. He saw a ladder that led up to a sleeping loft. Up there was the window where Ted had seen movement.

Chinook came back from his rambling exploration, then reared up, with his front feet on the loft ladder. A deep growl rumbled in his chest.

Scott tried to call district headquarters on the radio. It was after office hours, he knew, but Pete sometimes worked late.

Receiving no answer, he tried the Forest Service office at Emerald Lake, and there he got an answer.

He spoke loud enough to be heard inside the chalet. 'I'm at the cabins near Wildcat Falls. There's been a break-in, and someone is still here. Relay by phone to the sheriff's office, Gateway.'

'Will do!'

Moments later a scared voice came from the loft. 'We'll come down, but get that dog away from us.'

Scott doubted that Chinook would bite anyone, but he said, 'Come here, killer!' He held the husky by the collar while two young men came down the ladder.

It turned out that they were local men. Barbara and the twins knew them both. While cruising in the aspens above the cabins on a borrowed snowmobile, they had seen the machines come out of Crystal Basin in a long string. After a time they decided that, as late as it was, no more snowmobiles would show up.

On the spur of the moment, one of them had suggested breaking into the chalet and spending the night there, just for the fun of it. They had just got the gas heaters lit and the place warmed up, when they heard Scott and the others coming.

The lock on the door they had forced was so broken as to be useless. That appeared to be all the damage the two had done.

Scott made them turn the gas off at the tank outside. He had them jam the back door shut with a magazine as a wedge to keep the door from blowing open.

And then he told them, 'You fellows go on ahead and turn yourselves in to the sheriff. It could go a little easier with you if he doesn't have to come after you.'

The two culprits took off on the White Charger.

'They've never been in any trouble that I ever heard of before this,' Barbara said. 'It surprised me when you called us over to the porch and I saw who they were.'

'They're scared,' Scott said. 'I hope this one deal cures them.'

'Boy, oh, boy! You sure find trouble every time you go out, don't you, Scott?' Ted said. 'You arrest guys for killing elk, you swipe girls, and you catch burglars. How come you're always in the middle of everything?'

'Just lucky, I guess.' He certainly had fallen into some unusual experiences, and none of them was any help towards getting done the job that he had been sent to do, Scott thought glumly.

Ted got an impish, teasing look on his tanned face. 'The rest of the way down, Barb, you won't have to hug him so much, like you did up there on the curves.'

'I was merely holding on.'

'Oh, no, Barb! You were hugging him, all right. Wasn't she, Bob?'

'It was awful,' Bob said piously.

'Let's get out of here,' said Scott, 'before I drown both of them in the snow.'

Chapter 6

BIG UTE

A few days later Scott reported by phone to the regional forester, who asked what progress he was making.

'About all I can say so far is that I'm getting acquainted with the situation,' Scott said. 'Pete Bartholomew has called a public meeting for everyone interested in snowmobiling, a week from today. I can tell you more after that.'

'Is there anything I can do to help?'

'I can't think of anything at the moment.'

That afternoon in Pete's office, Scott studied a copy of the byelaws of the Silver Peaks Snowmobile Club. That was a large and successful organisation from towns close to the Platoro National Forest.

Tommy Thompson had prepared two hundred copies of the papers for distribution at the meeting.

'The district ranger over there says the club is really doing a great job of eliminating a lot of the same problems we have here,' Thompson said. 'Maybe it isn't the whole answer,' he added, 'but it sure is helping in that forest.'

The routine organisational details were very much like those of any kind of club, Scott noted. What interested him most was the article outlining a code of behaviour for club members:

> . . . good sportsmanship . . . operating in accordance with local, state, and federal regulations . . . respecting private property and national forest lands . . .

It was simple enough, Scott thought, but it covered just about everything. There were no provisions for throwing a member out of the club for violating a regulation. That was good.

It was much better to have a positive approach to behaviour, like the group of young snowmobilers at the lake, Scott thought. The day before, Jerry Wayne had seen Pete and told him that the group would take up a collection to pay for the ruined table, even though none of them had been the first one to build a fire on it.

'Well, what do you think of it?' Thompson asked, after Scott had finished studying the papers.

'It's all right, Tommy. What chance do you think we'll have of pulling a big crowd at the meeting?'

'I'm hopeful. Even if we don't get a big crowd, if we do get most of the key people who can swing the thing, we'll be all right.' Thompson glanced at the window.

'Hey! It's snowing! That reminds me – I've got to go up to the ski course tomorrow. How about coming along?'

'Skiing?'

'You can, if you want to. I've got to make a routine check of operations.'

'I won't be able to take Lassie.'

'Sure you will. Leave her in the pickup when we get to the course.'

Over in the corner, Lassie heard her name and came over to see what was going on. As Pete had said, she was not happy as an office dog, and now she seemed to sense that Scott was going out.

The Big Ute ski course was a mile off the highway that crossed Elk Pass. The parking lots were jammed with cars, and the four lifts appeared to be running at full capacity.

The snow of the day before had put down about six inches. During the night the storm had passed, and now it was a beautiful, sparkling day.

Thompson parked in the space reserved for employees, close to the lodge. Scott rolled one window down a little and left Lassie in the cab.

Getting his skis from the bed of the truck, Scott looked at the long runs on the slopes, where tiny figures were weaving back and forth. 'Which run do you recommend, Tommy?'

'That depends on how you ski. That one clear over to the left is Humpty Dumpty, for beginners. If you think you're a champion, try War Chief. That's the lift with the green towers.'

Scott went up on War Chief. It was a fast, smooth-running lift. At the twentieth tower, he thought he was close to the top, but the line then went over a minor crest, and he saw fifteen or sixteen more towers ahead.

When he dipped out of the chair at the top, he was on the spine of the Menzies Range, at this point about 11,000 feet above sea level.

The ski run was somewhere off to his left; he had caught only glimpses of it on the way up, and now he had a moment of misgiving, wondering if he had bitten off more than he could chew. Though he had confidence in his ability to ski, he had not been on the slopes since the previous winter.

He swung off the trail where it curved through the rocks on the crest. When he removed his skis and stuck them upright in the snow, it struck him that the top of the run, very narrow and almost icy, was made of snow that had been carried from somewhere else. The rest of the summit around him was scoured bare by the wind.

He climbed up on the rocks to look at the mountains. It was an awesome view. Both south and north of him were great peaks that ripped the sky at more than 14,000 feet.

From where he was the mountain ran west in a spur for about two miles before crashing headlong into the main run of the Menzies. Just south of the junction was a slanting crest that was heavy with overhanging snow.

From his study of maps, he reasoned that the avalanche area that Pete had posted with warning signs was close to that junction.

As Scott stood there for a few moments longer in the freezing wind, he half expected to see the tiny shape of a snowmobile crawling along the long, swooping snowfield below the distant ridge.

All this time the lift behind him had been disgorging skiers. None of them was interested in scenery. With their skis scraping on the icy strip, they all went skimming around the curve and dipped away towards the trees below.

'Hey, Scott! What are you doing up there?'

Scott turned to see two boys in knit face masks.

They had pulled off the run and were staring up at him.

'You afraid to ski down?'

The ski clothes and the masks made them almost unrecognisable, but there was no mistaking the voices – the Snow Dust Twins.

Scott climbed down. 'Well, the Abominable Snowmen! You two get everywhere.'

'Ted wanted to go snowmobiling,' Bob said, 'but we couldn't find anyone to drive the truck, so we came up here on the ski bus. What were you doing up there on the rocks?'

'Just looking.'

The boys glanced at each other, and Scott saw the amused expression in their eyes.

'Some people ride the lift back,' Ted suggested.

Scott smiled. 'Chicken people?'

'Yeah!'

Two young girls went by. They were wobbly and wide on the turn. One of them yelled, 'Now, wait for me, Sue! Oh, why did we ever come up here?'

'You *could* ride the lift down, Scott,' Bob said. 'It's better than breaking your legs.'

Scott kept a straight face. 'Maybe I can make it.'

'We'll take you down,' Ted offered. 'You've got to know what you're doing on War Chief, and you've got to be careful. Skiing is no fun, you know, if you're always busting something or running into a tree.'

Scott was putting his skis on. 'I agree. I feel the same way about snowmobiling, Ted. Don't you?'

'That's a little different.'

Scott leaned forward to test his binders. He jabbed his poles into the icy run. 'I'm as ready as I'll ever be.'

Ted took the lead, with Scott in the middle. Scott

was not fooling on the first dip, a hill of about 42 degrees, when he almost went into a windmill.

'Stay left!' Bob yelled. 'Left!'

It was good advice. Scott recovered in time to avoid a stretch of thin snow where rocks were showing. He was never out of control or off-balance again.

At the bottom of several steep pitches, they found skiers who had piled up. Ted always stopped to inquire about injury and need of help. They found no one who said he was hurt or needed aid.

For about half the run, Bob was yelling at Scott and then he apparently decided that Scott was doing all right and quit giving him advice.

Ted stopped where a narrow run began through trees. 'Take it easy here,' he said. 'There's not much room to get around the stupid girls who are always piled up right in the middle of the track.'

It was a tight run, and it dipped over several humps that made it impossible to see very far ahead. Ted was right. Suddenly they came upon the same two girls they had seen at the top, both of them sprawled out in the middle of the course.

Ted shot out into the soft snow to get around them. 'You all right?' he yelled.

'Yes!' one of the girls shouted angrily.

'Then quit lying there, and get out of the way!'

At the bottom of the run, Bob shook his head at Scott. 'You're a faker. You can really ski.'

'I wasn't faking, Bob. I'm always a little scared of a hill I haven't been on before.' Scott unsnapped his binders.

'Aren't you going up again with us?' Ted asked.

'Not today.'

Knowing that Thompson would be busy for some time, Scott drove the pickup back towards the highway. He stopped and let Lassie exercise for a while beside the snowbanks on the area road.

Then he went back to the crowded lounge of the ski chalet for coffee. There he met Bill Jackman, the assistant manager of the ski area, who mistook him for an inspector.

'I just came along with Thompson for the ride. I *am* interested in the avalanche area southwest of here, however.'

Jackman took Scott to a huge aerial map on the wall and swept his finger along the curving ridge that Scott had seen from the top of War Chief.

'That's it,' Jackman said. 'We've posted it, and you guys have posted it, but a few knotheads still go over there from the top of Bright Arrow run. It's not very far across to the slide area.' Jackman shook his head. 'As soon as they turn the wrong way at the bull wheel up there, they have to go around a Forest Service barricade covered with warning signs. A few of them *still* do it.'

Always a few adventurous idiots, Scott thought. 'Can snowmobiles get into the slide area?'

'Oh, yes. Our use permit extends clear to the top of the range, so that avalanche area is included. When snowmobilers show up here on the course, naturally, we don't let them even unload their machines.

'But there's no way to stop them from going back to the highway, on up Elk Pass, and then into that slide country over an old logging road. A few of them do that.'

Jackman went on to explain that for a long time the safety man at the top of Bright Arrow had been provided with a bullhorn. Whenever he saw anyone turn towards the slide area, or anyone in it, he ran out of the control shack and ordered the trespasser to clear out.

'Then a state inspector came along and saw him do that one day,' Jackman said. 'He gave us orders to keep the safety operator within reach of the emergency switches in the control shack at all times.' He shrugged. 'We gave up the bullhorn idea.'

The state inspector was right, Scott thought. The safety man's first duty was to skiers on the chair lift. If something went wrong with the equipment, or if he saw a skier getting into trouble unloading, the safety man had to be there to cut power instantly.

Later, going back to the highway with Thompson, Scott asked, 'Can you see the avalanche area from the highway?'

'No, you can't. I'll take you up that way, though, and show you where an old road runs over towards the avalanche area.'

It was about two miles above the ski course road. The highway was ploughed out very wide at the point.

On the old logging road that went up steeply through the trees was the track of a snowmobile. No trailer or pickup was parked on the wide shoulder, and the track was blown partly full of snow.

No one was on the old road now, but a snowmobile had been there perhaps two days before.

'I don't know how you keep jerks like that from deliberately inviting death,' Thompson said.

'Maybe we'll find out at the meeting.'

Chapter 7

FAILURE

The meeting was set for eight o'clock in the evening at Community Hall, in a room that would hold four hundred people. Thompson had joked about the size of the hall earlier in the day. 'I doubt that we'll fill it, but you have to think big.'

Light snow was falling when Scott drove into the parking lot with Lassie. He had just got out of the jeep when Fritz Pettigrew arrived with his sons and Chinook.

'Hey, Scott!' Ted shouted. 'Are you going to let Lassie stay out here with Bob and me? We'll come in when the meeting starts.'

'Day or night,' Pettigrew said, 'they'd rather be running around in the snow than anything else in the world. I think I'll palm them off on the Royal Canadian Mounted Police. I hear the Mounties are using snowmobiles now, instead of dogsleds.'

'Hey!' Bob cried. 'We'd like that! How old do you have to be?'

'Forget it.' Pettigrew grinned at Scott, and then he waved his hands at the boys. 'All right, stay out here and play until you freeze.'

'Go ahead, Lassie,' Scott said. He knew that she

would come barking at the door when it got too snowy or cold for her.

Thompson and Pete with Jim Benton, the round-faced Glory dealer, were waiting inside. Benton was to be the chairman.

'Now, how do you want to handle this?' he asked. 'Shall I push right along towards getting clubs organised, or shall we first go into some of the problems we discussed in Pete's office?'

'I'd suggest that we review the problems, maybe just briefly, and then feel out the attitude towards forming clubs,' Thompson said.

He glanced at the clock. They still had twenty minutes before meeting time, but Thompson was worried. He had called or talked to fifty or more snowmobilers, had the meeting announced on radio and in the newspaper – in fact, he had done about everything he could to get the snowmobilers to attend.

Bill Warner, the state fish and game warden, and Sheriff Briscoe showed up a few minutes later. Briscoe looked around the empty hall and said, 'I thought this was a public meeting.'

'Give them time,' Pete said.

Cars and jeeps began to arrive soon afterwards, and people straggled into the room, stomping the snow from their feet on the mat at the door.

Three of the snowmobile dealers who had not been present at the first meeting showed up. Barbara Vogel and Jerry Wayne came in together, followed by six or seven people whom Scott recognised from having met them at Blue Lake.

For a while there was a fairly steady stream of people. Scott saw Brad Parris, one of the men Warner had arrested at the old line camp.

Benton waited until ten minutes after eight before

calling the meeting to order. By then there were fifty-three people present. That was pretty good, Scott thought.

'The purpose of this meeting is to review some of the problems that we are creating with snowmobiles and to see what we can do about them,' Benton said. 'We have with us officials from the Forest Service, the county, and the state, so I'm going to ask each one of them to summarise his particular grievance.'

That part of it went about the same as before. Pete spoke for the Forest Service, and Briscoe and Warner outlined the problems they were having with snowmobiles.

'Any comment?' Benton asked.

Brad Parris stood up. 'I think we all understand the problems well enough, but here's the thing about it: in any group of people, there's always going to be a few outlaws, and –'

'You ought to know, Brad!' a man said.

There was laugher. Parris took it good-naturedly, though he glanced quickly at Scott and Warner to see if they were laughing, too.

'What I'm saying,' Parris resumed, 'is that there'll always be a few people getting out of line. We all know what the real purpose of this meeting is.

'It's to soft-soap us into forming clubs. Personally, I don't see any need of that. Say we do organise. Then what? Are we supposed to chase down the bad guys that throw gum wrappers around the national forests, or the ones that chase elk, or the sneak thieves that bust into cabins?'

'Will someone answer that?' Benton asked.

Barbara Vogel stood up. 'I'm sure that the aim of the people who spoke a while ago is not to get us to form clubs as law enforcement agencies.

'It's a matter of attitude, I think. Let me explain that. About twenty-five of us are in a group that does things together. We're not a club, but we do try to observe fundamental safety rules.

'Here's another example: we frown on anyone who throws litter around. We don't quote a rule to him; we just make it clear that this is wrong. If someone wants to go barrelling off by himself into dangerous country, we don't order him not to go, but we impress on him the risks involved.'

Parris waved his hands. 'Okay, you're the goody-goody girls. You don't need a club, so it must be the rest of us that the fish and game warden and the Forest Service want to convert into decent citizens.'

He was being unfair, and he probably knew it, Scott thought, but that matter of the game violation was sticking in his craw.

Sitting in the front row, Scott had worked his chair around so that he could see the faces in the audience. It seemed to him that Parris's talk had made a strong impression, especially on some of the men.

Chairman Benton sensed that, too. He called on Pettigrew, in an effort to hear a friendly voice in support of clubs.

'As a dealer, I think I would be helped if we had well-run snowmobile clubs,' Pettigrew said, 'and they might help clear up some of the problems we've heard about.'

He could have done better than that, Scott thought.

'Of course, it's up to the snowmobilers themselves,' Pettigrew went on. 'I don't want to assume the position of telling them what they ought to do.'

Pete leaned over to whisper to Scott. 'He sure turned lukewarm. I think I know why.'

The other dealers were not much help, either. Two

of them said they did not know enough about clubs to voice an opinion, while the third one merely repeated what Pettigrew had said already.

'Jerry Wayne?' Scott asked Pete. 'Is that the trouble?'

Pete nodded. 'I'd say so.'

Wayne ran a large garage. Among other things, he was the dealer for a popular foreign sports car and motorbikes. He also had a special department for servicing and repairing snowmobiles. Of the five snowmobile dealers in town, only Benton had full facilities for servicing the product he sold.

Even Pettigrew, who sold more snowmobiles than anyone else, contracted a large part of his follow-up work on the machines to Jerry Wayne.

Scott tried his best to be fair in his thinking, but it seemed to him that Wayne must have dropped a few hints, here and there, to the effect that he did not favour organising clubs.

The expression of opinion continued, and there were several people who made strong speeches in favour of clubs.

But, studying the audience, Scott noted signs of flagging interest. Everyone had been given a copy of the byelaws of the Silver Peaks club. Now the papers were disappearing into pockets, and people seemed to be getting restless.

Pete, too, was worried. 'Shall I mention a few restrictions we *could* clamp on?'

'I wouldn't do that,' Scott advised. 'It would only strengthen the idea that we're trying to force them into forming clubs.'

'After the next one gets through talking, let's try a coffee break,' Thompson suggested. 'Maybe that will loosen things up.'

The Snow Dust Twins came in with Lassie and Chinook while the meeting was temporarily adjourned to let people stretch and gather around the big coffee urn. From the amount of snow the dogs and the boys got rid of in the tiled entrance, Scott knew that the storm outside was a big one.

He went over to tell Lassie to stay at the back of the hall. Brad Parris followed him.

'I just thought I'd say hello to the warden,' Parris said, grinning. 'She's a better sniffer-outer than Warner ever could be.'

Parris patted Lassie on the head. 'You and me have got nothing against each other, have we?'

Lassie seemed to agree, and Parris gave Scott a grin as he walked away.

Over at the coffee supply, Thompson was talking to Jerry Wayne, apparently working on him to speak in favour of snowmobile clubs.

A few people drifted away during the coffee break, going out into the storm.

When the meeting resumed, the Snow Dust Twins listened for a while, and then they began to nod in the heat of the room. Lassie and Chinook lay where they had been ordered to stay. They licked the ice from between their paws, and then they, too, began to doze.

The key to the whole plan was Wayne, Scott thought. If Thompson had done any good with his effort to gain Wayne's support, then maybe the meeting would get somewhere.

Benton asked Wayne to state his views.

'Personally, I'm not interested in any kind of formal organisation,' Wayne said. 'It's all right, I suppose, for those who like that sort of thing.

'As Barbara said a while ago, we have a small group

that gets along well together without eight sheets of written byelaws. That's as far as I'm interested in going.'

Scott saw a dozen people nod their agreement.

Benton was still trying. 'All right, maybe the club idea is the wrong approach to the problems we all admit. Has anyone a better suggestion that will prevent snowmobiling from ending up under state and federal restrictions – which we snowmobilers don't want?'

'I think it's up to the individual snowmobiler,' a man said. 'Those of us who respect the national forests and private property and don't chase game and so forth – we can't be held responsible for the few who do these things.'

'Oh, yes, we can,' Benton said. 'If we don't make some effort to regulate our own sport, you can rest assured that we'll be regulated.'

The meeting began to dissolve into arguments that had nothing to do with snowmobiling.

By the time Benton restored order, more people had left. The best the chairman could do then was to appoint a committee to explore the subject of snowmobile clubs and to report back at the next meeting, which would have to be announced later.

Afterwards, when the only ones left were those who had been at the first meeting in Pete's office, and the Snow Dust Twins who were sound asleep in their chairs, Thompson shook his head ruefully.

'About as many as I expected turned out, but we still didn't get anywhere,' he said. 'Should we have done more talking ourselves, sort of thrown in a few threats, say?'

Sheriff Briscoe's keen eyes were glinting with a touch of humour. 'No, you did about right, I'd say,

Tommy. For forty years I've seen meetings like this.

'You don't have any luck forcing people to do anything. Now, this little confab tonight was maybe better than you think. The loud voices always come from those who are against something, but I saw a lot of folks here tonight who didn't say much. Believe me, now they're thinking, turning the idea over in their heads. Maybe we got a little further than it appeared.'

Pettigrew was trying to wake the twins. 'When they go, they go,' he said, 'and when they sleep – oh, boy!'

Scott had been thoroughly sold on the idea of snowmobile clubs, but now he began to examine the thought critically. 'Are we on the right track, pushing this club business?'

Benton spread his hands. 'You heard the only answer I got when I asked that same question a while ago. Have you got another answer?'

Scott shook his head.

'How many men and how much money would it take to create a force to control the situation we have?' the sheriff asked. He let that sink in, and then he said, 'We've already got the force: the snowmobilers themselves.

'All that's left is to get them to accept the responsibility. I think we're making progress, in spite of the way things went tonight. Speaking from my own selfish interests, if I could persuade just half of the snowmobilers to take a few minutes to check the summer homes they go past, before long it would be so risky for anyone to make a break-in that ninety-five per cent of my problem would be settled.'

Warner nodded. 'If we can ever sell the idea of

responsibility, then *all* our problems are going to be eased.'

'Right!' the sheriff said. 'By the way, Scott, I can understand why Brad Parris is a little teed off at you and Warner, but what did you do to Jerry Wayne? A few times tonight I noticed the two of you looking at each other like strange bulldogs.'

Pettigrew had finally shaken his sons awake. Ted heard the sheriff's question. He yawned and said, 'Old Scott, he sort of grabbed off Jerry's girl up at Blue Lake the other day. That's what he did.'

Bob was sleepy and cross. He gave his brother a shove. 'Aw, it wasn't like that at all. Scott didn't try to steal her. She tried to steal him.'

'One way or another, that explains it,' the sheriff said. 'Let's go home.'

They went out into a steady, heavy snowfall. Chinook thought it was wonderful. He loped around the parking lot like a pup. Lassie went straight to the jeep and waited for Scott to open the door.

Chapter 8

AVALANCHE

On his way up Elk Pass to check the snowslide area, Scott stopped once to make a test call on the radio Sheriff Briscoe had lent him.

He still had a Forest Service pack set, but it was on a different frequency. It was Briscoe's idea that Scott might again have reason to get in touch quickly with the sheriff's office.

The storm of two days before had left about thirty inches of new snow. Then there had been a day and night of intense cold. It was warmer now, but there was a feeling in the air that a new storm was on its way.

Lassie was looking ahead at the road with interest. She knew her little sled was on the trailer with the Rocket.

The sky was closing in above the mountains when Scott pulled over in the wide place near the old logging road that led to the avalanche area. A red pickup was parked there, and a state highway snowplough.

There were fresh marks of a snowmobile in the logging road.

'Did you see who went up that road?' Scott asked

the snowplough operator, who was making an adjustment on the plough.

'Just barely,' the man said. 'They were pulling into the timber when I got here. Looked like three kids. There was a big dog with them.'

'Blue snowmobiles?'

'Yeah, they were.'

Scott lost no time in getting started. The logging road followed a gulch with timbered sides that kept growing steeper and steeper. Before he reached the head of it, the tracks he was following left the road and angled up through the trees on his right.

Straight towards the avalanche area. Those crazy kids!

He came around the shoulder of the mountain spur and got a good look at the slide area, about a quarter mile beyond.

The great curving crest, with its overhanging cornice of snow, reared high above a long snowfield that swooped down like the side of a bowl, clear to the trees.

Sitting up in her trailer sled, Lassie whined at the sight of a dog racing along behind two blue snowmobiles. The ribbons of their tracks were laced across the snowfield in several places.

Scott stood up in the seat and yelled as loudly as he could. 'Get out of there!' Even as he shouted, he knew that the Snow Dust Twins and the third boy could not hear him above the noise of their engines.

They stopped at the far end. He shouted again, and still they did not hear him, though Chinook turned to look towards him. Lassie barked then, and the boys seemed to have heard the sound, for they began to look around.

They looked the wrong way, to the north and to

the east, towards the ski course. The bowl they were in made it impossible for them to determine from what direction the noise had come.

There was only one thing to do – go on over and chase them out of the dangerous area. The way Scott felt at the moment, he thought a sound spanking would be in order, too.

He grunted angrily as the tracks led him within ten feet of the avalanche warning signs.

The Skimmers were coming back across the snowfield. One, with only the driver on it, was breaking a new track high on the slope. The second one, with two boys on it, was following an already broken track lower down.

Chinook was coming along behind the lower machine.

The west wind was spinning streamers of snow off the crest. And then Scott saw a change in the pattern. Instead of drifting away before the wind, plumes of snow dust began to fall vertically.

Scott did not want to believe it was happening, but he saw it start. A section of the cornice, at least a hundred yards wide, plunged suddenly from the crest.

It struck the snowfield with a sullen, shocking thump that sent waves of air clear over to Scott, and then the upper end of the snowfield cracked in a jagged line.

The whole mass was moving. Huge chunks of crust beneath the new snow came thrusting up, turning, breaking. The only noise now was an enormous sighing sound as the tremendous mass of snow gained speed.

The lower snowmobile seemed to have a chance. The upper one turned, running straight downhill before the slide.

And then the whole scene was smothered by fine powder snow, thrown into the air by the concussion of the mighty force. Scott could see nothing of the two blue Skimmers.

He had stopped the Rocket, though he did not remember doing so. Lassie was excited, whining, moving from side to side in the trailer, as if to jump out. But she had learned her lesson about leaping into deep snow.

Scott tried the Forest Service radio first. He was in a dead spot, with the high ridge crowding him on the right. He got no answer to his call.

He was still trying when he heard shouts from the gloom of fine snow. There were at least two voices.

'Are you all right?' he yelled.

The two voices answered together, and he could not tell what they said. The snow dust was beginning to clear. He caught a glimpse of two white-covered figures beside a blue machine.

And still he got no response to his radio call.

In desperation he tried the radio the sheriff had given him. It had less range than the other one, he knew.

'Gateway, Unit one-two-three-six.'

He tried three times. There was no acknowledgement. The ridge was blocking transmission.

He called again. This time he got an answer, not from the sheriff's office in Gateway, but from the operator of the snowplough on the highway.

'Will relay message, one-two-three-six.'

Now Scott could see the slide area clearly. It was an awesome scene of jumbled snow that had funnelled clear down into the trees.

He heard a voice that broke plaintively. 'Ted's gone! Help us!'

Scott gave his message to the snowplough operator. 'Unit one-two-three-six to Gateway. Avalanche in slide area of old logging road! Two boys safe. Pettigrew boy buried. Send help – hurry!'

Help would come quickly, he was sure, but a human being under that mass of snow, even if uninjured, had only about fifteen minutes of life. At least two of those minutes were already gone!

Bob and an older boy whom Scott did not know came scrambling to meet him as he ran the Rocket up to the edge of the slide.

From under the seat, Scott took a telescoping steel rod. It was very much like the antenna of a car radio, except larger. He ran it out to its full eight feet.

The older boy, whom Bob called Benny, was scared and crying. Bob did not look too good himself, but there was tough fibre in him. 'Shut up, Benny! We've got to find Ted and Chinook!'

Walking on the slide was no easy matter. In places the compressed snow held them up, but there were soft spots that had to be avoided.

Scott took the middle, judging as best he could the line that Ted had been running when the slide caught him. He put one boy on each side.

Crawling, leaping from one slab to another, Lassie worked her way along the slide.

'He'll be all right, won't he, Scott?' Bob asked, pleading.

'Keep looking.'

There was little the boys could do, except to look. Scott used the rod to probe, shoving it down as far as he could as they worked towards the trees.

There was no way to know how far the slide had carried Ted, or whether he had been caught on the Skimmer with his legs astride the engine.

'We've got to find him!' Bob cried.

'Keep trying.' It was all the advice Scott could give the boys at this point.

The way Ted had been moving when Scott last saw him, it seemed that he might have outrun the slide. 'How far towards the trees was he when you saw him last?'

'He only got to the deep trail,' Bob said. 'The skis dug in there and flipped him. I could just barely see him then.'

Scott kept working his probe. 'You saw him thrown out?'

'I don't know. I could just barely see the Skimmer rolling over, and then all that fine snow made everything dark.'

Much more than five minutes had passed.

Strange things happen in snowslides, Scott thought. A person was sometimes fortunate enough to be trapped in an air pocket that would sustain him for a long time, but that was the exception; most people trapped in a slide as big as this one were killed.

Scott worked the probe and prayed for the exception.

He had forgotten Lassie, until she began to bark excitedly. She was behind them and off to one side. They scrambled over to her as fast as they could.

She was digging in soft snow between slabs of crust.

'She's found Ted!' Bob shouted. He and Benny threw themselves flat and began to dig furiously with their hands. 'I can feel him! He's warm!'

They were too far north of where Ted had been, Scott knew. He was not surprised a few moments later when Bob, who was sprawled on the snow on his side, reaching down with one hand, got an odd look on his face and said, 'It's Chinook! I can feel him moving!'

'Dig him out.' Scott went back to the middle of the slide and on down towards the trees.

Too much time had passed, but maybe there was a chance for the exception. He was doing all that was possible for one man. He kept working, feeling down into the snow with the rod, judging what he was encountering by the resistance.

The rod was finding nothing but snow. Even when his hand was buried, Scott knew he was reaching down only eight feet. In places the slide was at least twenty feet deep!

He heard Lassie barking happily. Glancing around, he saw Chinook, and the husky seemed to be in good condition.

'Bring the dogs down here!' Scott yelled.

Lassie had found Chinook under the snow. Just maybe . . . The cold fact of the matter was that Chinook had not been buried very deeply, and he had been near the edge of the slide, where the snow was loose.

It was different farther out in the slide where weight had compressed the snow. In some places it was so hard that Scott had difficulty forcing the steel rod down into it.

Lassie found Ted's black Cossack hat. They did not know exactly where she had picked it up, but the boys insisted on digging where they thought she had found it.

First Scott probed the area with the rod. He touched nothing that felt like a human being, but Bob and Benny were still set on digging, though they had only their hands to work with.

Scott went back to the middle of the slide. It had

tailed out in a swale that ran towards the ski course. This run was wider than previous ones, for it had spread to catch trees on both sides, growth that apparently had been untouched for a long time.

The first help came from the Big Ute ski patrol, four men who skied in from the top of Bright Arrow Run with a toboggan and other equipment.

From his glassed-in hut at the top of Bright Arrow, the safety operator had seen the slide. His call to the lodge was just minutes ahead of Sheriff Briscoe's call for help to the same place, after he had received Scott's relayed message.

Scott lined up the four men, and they all began to probe, still working towards the lower end of the slide.

'When the call came, we had a man with a broken leg on War Chief and a heart attack case in the parking lot,' Cliff Hardesty said. 'That's why we didn't get here sooner.'

Scott looked at his watch. It was almost a half hour since he had seen the cornice giving way.

'How long?' Hardesty asked, and Scott told him.

'We won't find anyone alive in this mess.'

Still digging where the hat had been, Bob and Benny heard the words.

'We will too find him alive!' Bob shouted. 'You shut up, Hardesty! We'll find him!'

And then Bob began to cry.

Scott left his rod sticking in the snow and went over to him.

'You think we'll find him, don't you, Scott?'

'There's always hope.' Scott put his arm around the boy for a moment.

The dogs had lost interest in the futile digging and had gone on down the slide. Glancing back at the sky above the crest, Scott saw that the storm which had been threatening was very close.

Six more helpers came from the ski course, among them Dr Walter Inman. It was just beginning to snow.

Accompanied by Dr Inman, Scott took the boys back to the snowmobiles. Bob's face was strained and tear streaked. 'We'll find him, won't we, Scott?'

'We'll do our best.' The slide was beyond the end of the ridge that had blocked radio transmission before, and now Scott got a quick response when he tried the Forest Service pack set.

'Still looking for Ted Pettigrew,' he told Pete's secretary. 'We've got ten volunteers from the ski course, but we need more help.'

'Pete and Tommy are on their way with five men. The sheriff is rounding up snowmobilers. Any injuries?'

'Negative. Dr Inman is here, and he'll stay as long as needed. Has Pettigrew been notified?'

'Affirmative. The sheriff called him.'

Dr Inman was giving the boys hot coffee. He glanced at Scott and said, 'I'll stay with them.'

It was snowing hard as Scott went back down the slide to direct the search. Hard logic told him that it was now a futile task, but they had to keep trying as long as there was any hope at all; and, after that, they still had to find Ted.

At dusk the searchers had turned up nothing – no trace of Ted. By then the slide was jammed with snowmobiles. Fritz Pettigrew and Jerry Wayne had hauled in portable power generators. The lights made a strange glow in the falling snow.

There were arctic tents pitched on the surface of the slide, and in one of them Dr Inman had put Bob and Benny to bed in sleeping bags. Chinook was in the tent with them.

The voices of the searchers were strangely muted by the storm. There were at least sixty men, by Scott's estimate. Out on the highway, an extra snowplough had been sent up the pass to make room for the parked vehicles, some of which had been left partly on the road. Sheriff Briscoe had assigned a man to move the cars as fast as the plough cleared space.

Scott had not seen Lassie for some time, though she had been coming back to him at intervals, as if to make sure that he was still around.

Now she nudged against him as he stood under a slanting tarpaulin at the coffee station with Jim Benton and Pete.

'Too bad she couldn't have found the boy instead of the dog,' Benton said. He shook his head. 'Did you see Pettigrew's face a while ago?'

'Yeah.' The gasoline engines on the generators were making a steady barking sound. A snowmobile came up the trail from the highway, its headlights throwing a thin beam in the murk of falling snow.

The driver found the trail blocked with other machines. 'Give me some help with this food, somebody!' he yelled.

Oh, yes, Scott thought bitterly, the rescue operation was a big deal. Everyone jumped to get in on it and do whatever he could. But where were they when you tried to get something started that could have prevented the need for a search and rescue operation such as this?

He was dead tired, and he was hard hit thinking of Ted – and he had seen the stricken expression on Pettigrew's face when he first looked at the slide and saw the immensity of it and had to face the fact that one of his sons was somewhere under it. It never should have happened, but it had. And now they had to find him.

Wearily Scott went back to join the other searchers. Lassie was beside him for a while; then she disappeared into the gloom beyond the lights. And the snow kept falling heavily.

Chapter 9

LONG CHANCE

About midnight the searchers gave up for the night. The snowfall was so dense by then that the lights made only a feeble glow. About half of the men went home.

Scott kicked and tramped snow around the Rocket until he had a fairly level place. He had put the protective cover on the machine some time before, and now he used a large plastic sheet to make a slanting shelter over his sleeping bag beside the snowmobile.

Lassie did not think much of the arrangement. She stood outside for several minutes after Scott crawled in, and then she nosed inside and snuggled up beside Scott.

It was a snug shelter. It became even more snug several hours later, when the weight of snow built up and collapsed the sheet on the sleepers. Lassie was gone like a shot.

She pawed at the snow on the covering, barking frantically, trying to dig Scott out from beneath the crackling plastic. He was all right and would have stayed right where he was, but Lassie was sure he was buried and in great danger. She finally routed him out.

In the dreary light of dawn, Scott saw that it was still snowing. A few other sleepers, in tents and under makeshift shelters, had been roused by Lassie's excited barking. They, too, crawled out.

A small group had rigged more canvas and plastic at the coffee station and had kept the gas stove going all night. Pettigrew was here, looking pale and drawn.

Brad Parris was drinking coffee. He poured a cup for Scott and held it out. 'Rough night.'

Scott saw a man with a stubble of dark beard peering from a sleeping bag. For a moment he could not place him, and then he knew: Oscar Renfrow, one of the men with Parris when Warner had arrested them.

Pettigrew said, 'What're the chances, Scott?'

They all knew what he meant, but no one cared to give him the answer. Scott said, 'All we can do now is hope. Snowslides sometimes do freakish things.'

'The ski course offered to send a bulldozer,' Pettigrew said. 'What do you think?'

'It would take three days for him to fight his way in here,' Parris said. 'Maybe later, but now, while there's still an outside chance . . . ' He did not finish.

He took a sandwich from a box on a folding table, the legs of which were set on round pads of plywood to keep them from sinking into the snow. Parris offered the sandwich to Lassie, but she would not touch it until Scott said, 'It's all right, Lassie.'

Scott ate one of the cold sandwiches and had another cup of coffee. Renfrow got out of the sleeping bag. 'Well, we still have to keep trying.'

Pettigrew took a deep breath. 'No matter what, we've got to find him.'

Bob and Benny and Chinook arrived a few moments later. 'You boys take the Skimmer and go on home,' Pettigrew said. 'Benny, you do have a licence to drive a car, don't you?'

'Yes, sir.' Benny looked at his feet.

'All right,' Pettigrew said. 'It wasn't your fault, Benny. If they hadn't got you to drive for them, they would have got someone else. Go on home now, both of you. I'll keep Chinook here.'

'What'll I tell Mom?' Bob asked.

For an instant Pettigrew almost broke. He recovered with an effort and pointed to a pack set radio. 'The sheriff has kept her informed. All you can tell her is your end of it.'

Pettigrew put his arm around his son for a moment. 'Go on now, Bob.'

Crying, Bob and Benny walked away through the falling snow.

Scott led the men who were ready towards the lower end of the slide. Chinook made his usual plunging, powerful progress through the newly fallen snow. Lassie was having a little difficulty following him.

Both dogs disappeared into the storm.

The slabs of hard crust standing on end under the fresh snow made going very difficult, and the dim light made it impossible to judge the unevenness. Stumbling, sometimes falling, Scott and a few others went back to work. Soon afterwards they were joined by other men who had stayed overnight.

About half of those who had left the night before returned during the morning. If the snow continued, Scott knew that they would have to give up the search.

As it was, even the longest aluminium probe poles were not reaching anywhere close to the bottom of the jumbled mess.

It was after ten o'clock when a man called, 'I think I've got the snowmobile!'

They gathered around him. More probes went down until, by feel and by the outlines of the object below, the searchers know they were above the Skimmer.

By measurement on the probes, it was down fourteen feet, almost in the middle of the slide.

'Bring the shovels over here!' Pettigrew yelled. He knew as well as Scott that Ted had been thrown from the snowmobile, and because of the great difference in weight, it was unlikely that Ted and the machine would be anywhere close together.

'Dig it out,' Scott said. There were enough men to do that, and still enough more to go on searching farther down the slide.

Dr Inman came over to where Scott was working. 'You could miss him by an inch and never know it.'

Scott nodded. 'We're trying to follow a pattern, in grids five feet square. That's pretty tight, but still we could miss him. And our longest rod is only sixteen feet.'

'It's getting close to twenty-four hours now, isn't it?'

'People have survived longer than that under the snow,' Scott said.

'I'm with you on that. The boys told me he had insulated coveralls under his parka, insulated rubber packs, a wool mask, and warm gloves. It's a matter of whether he lodged in an area with an air space. I've fallen into a few soft spots scrambling around this mess – once almost to my ears. Between those big slabs I hit one place with a fair sized cavity.'

They were not trying to deceive each other or to raise false hopes. They both knew that the chance that Ted was still alive was very slim, but there was a chance. Until they knew for sure, one way or the other, they chose to be hopeful.

Twenty-four hours after the slide had run, many of the searchers quit. The storm was continuing as if there would never be an end to it. A man shook his head and said, 'It'll be summer before we ever find him.'

The diggers got down to the Skimmer by means of a long, sloping ramp. Each man in the line shovelled snow back to the worker behind him. The snowmobile was jammed so tightly that they had to hack the snow away with shovels to free it. They put a line on it and tied three snowmobiles together to pull it up the ramp. It was badly damaged.

Now the incline led to a hole fourteen feet deep. Pettigrew wanted to tunnel out from the bottom of it, but Pete talked him out of it. The hole was too dangerous. Neither could it be left open. Blinded by the storm a man might stumble into it. Pete ordered it filled up again.

To some that was the last glimmer of hope. They had seen how closely packed the snow was around the machine, and they knew that no one could have survived down there.

Scott's constantly thinning crew got to the end of the slide with their probing, and there, where it had run out of force in the little swale, the snow was piled forty feet high.

Pete came down to talk to Scott. 'I think we'd better call it off until after the storm. We're getting so much snow on the crest again that we could have another slide.'

Scott was dead tired and willing to admit it, but it

was not his weariness that made him agree with Pete; it was the hard logic of Pete's words.

Those who had stayed to the end – Parris, Renfrow, Dr Inman, Jerry Wayne, and about a dozen more – came trudging over when Pete called to them. They gathered around him, their clothing snow-plastered, their faces grim with the knowledge of failure.

While Pete talked to them briefly, Scott stood with slumped shoulders, staring into the storm. He kept seeing the face of a snub-nosed, grinning boy. Now there was only one Snow Dust Twin.

'Are you all right, Scott?' Dr Inman asked.

'Huh? Oh sure, sure. Just a little tired.' Scott looked around for Lassie. He knew that she was not very far away. Beyond the compacted area of the snow slide, the snow was too deep and soft for her.

Scott called to Lassie, and then he turned to join the other searchers walking up the slide.

Somewhere in the gloom of the storm, Lassie began to bark.

'Come on, Lassie!' Scott called.

She and Chinook caught up with Scott a few minutes later. Then they disappeared again, and, after a time, Lassie began to bark once more. She was somewhere on the north side of the swale, Scott thought.

There was a tone of great urgency in her voice, and it made Scott stop.

Parris came back to him. The two men stared at each other with questioning expressions, and Scott said, 'All right, let's go see what's got her stirred up.'

Lassie's signal led them across the slide to the thin edge of it, where it had caught some of the trees. She and Chinook were floundering around where the green branches of broken trees were barely showing above the snow.

As he got closer, it appeared to Scott that several small trees had been broken by the slide and had been jammed all together into one place.

The dogs were trying to get down through them. Chinook was in so deep that only the great plume of his bushy tail was showing.

'All right, let's have a look,' Scott said.

He had to make the dogs get out of the way before he could do anything. Lying on his stomach, Scott tried to peer down into the tangle of branches and loose snow. He could not see anything that would have excited the dogs.

Forcing the tough, springy boughs aside with his shoulders, he burrowed deeper. Snow from the new fall cascaded down and dribbled through the interlaced green branches.

Here on the edge of the slide there was not the packing that made other parts of the slide hard and solid. Still, there was plenty of snow mixed with the shattered trees.

There was open space down there, all right, Scott observed. But this was so far away from the middle of the slide, where Ted had been swept.

He wormed in deeper, scratching his face on the limbs. More snow caved in from the top and let in light. Scott thought he saw a splotch of red.

And then he saw brown wool that looked like a face mask. 'Ted? Ted?' he shouted, with a terrible fear that he would get no answer.

There was no answer. And then he saw two eyes blink open slowly in the face mask.

Head down, Scott was almost in a vertical position. Trying to back out of the hole, he found himself helpless, until Parris got him by the ankles and pulled him clear.

'It's Ted! He's alive!'

They both began to shout. Lassie and Chinook added their voices to the excitement.

It did not take the other searchers long to arrive. They came on the run, stumbling, falling, rising to drive on again.

They went down from the end to where Ted's feet were, working as fast as they could in relays. Dr Inman directed the last part of the excavation. After examination of Ted where he lay, when he was at last uncovered, the doctor had him moved carefully and gently on to a blanketed stretcher.

'Easy now! His right leg is broken.'

Dr Inman made another examination after they lifted the stretcher to the surface of the snow. Ted was unconscious. He had neither spoken nor moved during the rescue operation.

All Dr Inman would say was that his breathing and circulation seemed to be fair and that he would have to be in a hospital before the full extent of his injuries could be determined.

Minutes after Lassie and Chinook had led Scott and Parris to Ted, the sheriff had been notified by radio, and now there was an ambulance waiting on the highway.

Some of the volunteers who had come in fresh that morning hurried away with the stretcher. They would transfer Ted to a toboggan for the trip to the highway. Dr Inman said he would ski down behind them.

On the way back up the slide with Pete and Parris, Scott stopped to rest. The falling snow was so thick that he could not see to the far edge of the slide, over there where Lassie had found Chinook.

'Ted must have been running after he was dumped,' Scott said. 'They had one main track across the slide. He hit that; it flipped him. He must have run towards the north side. That's the only way I can account for his being so far over.'

'When he comes out of it, we'll know.' Parris brushed the snow from Lassie's head. 'Here's the old gal we can thank for that boy's life.' He looked at his bare hand. 'Doggone! I left my gloves down there. A ten-buck pair of gloves.'

He stood there debating with himself. He was as tired as anyone else, and now it seemed like a long way back through the snow to get the gloves.

'Tommy took your Rocket to bring in more supplies,' Pete said. 'That was just before you found the boy, so I called him and told him to leave it on the trailer and go home. You can ride out with me.'

'But Lassie – '

'I'll bring her out in my trailer,' Parris said. 'Renfrow and I may have to lash the sleeping bags on the snowmobiles to make room, but that won't be hard.'

Parris grinned when he saw Scott's hesitation. 'Do I look like a guy who would hold it against a dog for nailing me with illegal elk meat? A dog that just saved a boy's life?'

'You sure don't,' Scott said. 'I'll see you at the highway. And thanks.'

At the last moment, Parris decided to go back and get his gloves.

Only Parris's snowmobile was left when Pete and Scott were ready. Renfrow had started it and was now waiting for his partner. Scott explained about Lassie, and Renfrow said, 'Sure thing,' and began to make room for her in the trailer.

Lassie was already whining anxiously because

there was no trailer behind Pete's snowmobile. She jumped into Parris's trailer as soon as there was room.

'Stay there,' Scott said. He got on behind Pete, and they started out. They went only a short distance before Scott realised that the trail was so well packed that Lassie could have trotted on it.

Above a little cliff, someone had gone too high and then had skidded downhill, dragging snow so now there was a sloping place that reminded Scott somewhat of Heartthrob Point.

The Rocket slid a few feet towards the cliff, but it went on past, giving Scott a momentary jolt of unease. Pete drove on down to the highway.

Two men were running jumper cables from the battery of a jeep to the battery of Pettigrew's red pickup. They explained that Pettigrew had gone down in the ambulance with his son. One of them had promised to drive the pickup in, but, unable to start it, they had run the battery down.

Chinook was lying in the snow. He heard Scott's voice and came over to him. Thompson had already loaded one Rocket on the trailer. Scott and Pete ran the second one up and tied the sled across the seats.

'Go on in, why don't you?' Scott said. 'I may have to wait ten minutes more for Lassie.'

The two men got the pickup started just as Pete left. In a hurry because of the storm, one of them unclipped the cables, slammed the hood down, and yelled at the driver, 'Get it out of here while it's running!'

They completely forgot Chinook, and so did Scott, until it was too late. He shouted at them as they were going down the snowy highway, but they did not hear him.

No matter, he thought; he could take both dogs with him in the jeep. He did not have to wait long until Parris and Renfrow came down the logging road.

Lassie was not in the trailer.

Angry, and now suddenly distrustful of both men, Scott strode over to them. 'Where's Lassie?'

Parris and Renfrow twisted around to look at the trailer. 'She was there a minute ago.' Parris seemed to be genuinely surprised.

'I kept looking back for a while after we started,' Renfrow said. 'She was riding just fine.'

The storm, his own weariness, and the thought that he had made a bad mistake combined to create a great anger in Scott. He got control of himself before speaking.

'She'll be along,' he said. 'She can walk on that trail easily enough.'

'Sure she can,' Parris agreed.

They were idling the jeeps to get the heaters going, when Chinook made up his mind. Scott saw him bounding up the logging road. He leaped out and called to the husky. Chinook kept going up the trail. They waited fifteen minutes. Neither dog returned. A few cars went by at slow speed, with their chains clanking and their windshield wipers working hard.

Before long it would be night – and Lassie was out there somewhere in the snow.

Chapter 10

TRAPPED

Tired and wet from scrambling over the snowslide's uneven surface all day, Lassie was content to ride in the trailer behind Parris and Renfrow.

It was a shell-shaped sled with sloping sides, but there was a tent in the bottom that enabled her to brace her feet. The trail was smooth enough for her to lift one front paw to lick ice from between her pads.

The man riding behind the driver of the snowmobile kept looking back at her, but after a while, satisfied that she was doing all right, he stopped looking.

Everything was fine, until suddenly the snowmobile slewed on a tilted section of trail. The trailer, too, went sidewise.

It was not much of a skid, but Lassie had a keen recall of another place, where there had been ice and a deep canyon. All she could think of was to get out.

She jumped the wrong way.

For an instant she teetered on the edge of the little cliff, held by soft snow. Then the snow tumbled away, and she went over.

She sank out of sight in deep, soft snow at the

bottom of the cliff. By the time she struggled to the surface and began to bark, the snowmobile was far down the trail, and the noise of the engine covered her call for help.

The trail was up there. Lassie knew where it was. All she had to do was to get back to it. At the very base of the cliff, there was just a ribbon of clear ground, where wind had whistled around the rocks.

She got that far, pressed tightly against the cliff. Again she barked for help, but the snowmobile was now far away.

Working along the cliff, she reached one end of it, and there the snow blocked her again. She went back the other way and again encountered more snow than she could handle.

The trees were closer at that end of the rocks. Around the base of each one the snow dipped down in a little hollow. From being out with Scott in many places, Lassie had learned that those hollows were never as hard to move in as snow in open places.

She gathered her strength for a leap towards the nearest tree. Her jump carried her only part way, and she was buried again. After a tiring effort, she made it to the tree and rested there.

The next fir was only six or seven feet away, but it was still a fight to reach it. Going uphill was impossible, because there was a fifty-yard gap between groups of trees.

Lassie went the only way she could – downhill.

She had not gone very far and was resting under snow-laden boughs when she heard the whisking sound of paws on the trail somewhere above her. She barked.

The sounds stopped. She barked again. An instant

later she saw Chinook's wide face looking down at her from the trail.

In bounds and leaps, sometimes almost burrowing his way, Chinook came ploughing down to her. He tramped around under the tree, knocking snow from the boughs and licking Lassie's face.

Chinook was big and warm and full of tremendous energy. When he urged Lassie to follow him back uphill to the trail, she could not do it. She tried, but the grade was too steep, even with the husky breaking the way.

Lassie went back to the tree.

All right, Chinook seemed to say, *let's have it your way, then.*

He led the way downhill, from tree to tree. Wet and trembling, Lassie followed him. Even Chinook found the going difficult, but his huge feet and the long fur of his outercoat gave him flotation that Lassie lacked. His undercoat of fur, thick and fine and white, gave him body insulation to ward off the cold that was sapping Lassie's strength.

In the first surge of their going, they made a quarter mile, into a stand of timber. Shivering and nearly exhausted, Lassie lay down. Chinook stood beside her, whining, urging her to rise and follow him again.

He had been angling towards the highway. They could hear the engines of automobiles less than a mile away. Chinook knew where he was going, and he could have made it all the way. Though he could not understand why Lassie was not like him, he would not leave her. After a time, he lay down beside her. Lassie snuggled close to the warmth of his huge body.

It was getting close to night. The wind rose a little, drifting over the two dogs.

* * *

The wind was whipping snow in their faces as the three men, on two snowmobiles, went up the logging road again. Parris was angry with Renfrow for not keeping a better eye on Lassie while she was riding in the trailer.

'How did I know she was going to fall out?' Renfrow growled.

Scott was not in the best of humour, either, and he was deeply worried about Lassie. He was sure she could not have gone very far away from the trail. He kept telling himself that Chinook would find her.

They passed the icy place in a whirl of snow that was almost blinding. It was easy to miss seeing the marks where Chinook had left the beaten track in one great leap.

With their headlights turned on, they went all the way back to the snowslide. Scott whistled and called. There was no response.

The chopped-up area where snowmobiles had been and where men had tramped was already smoothing over with snow. Parris tried to find some sign that the dogs had been there recently.

Renfrow wiped melting snow from his dark beard-stubbled cheeks. 'We couldn't even see the husky's tracks near the highway. The snow covered them about as fast as he made them, so why do you think you can find tracks here?'

'I can try, can't I?' Parris was about out of patience with his partner.

'I don't think they came back here,' Scott said. He thought about the sloping place near the little cliff. Lassie had leaped out of the trailer at Heartthrob Point and at a couple of other places where the trailer slid or tipped.

But if she had jumped out at the cliff, she would have landed on the hard-packed trail and she could have gone on to the highway.

It was getting difficult to see. The headlights of the snowmobile were making only dull blobs of light.

'Let's go back and try – ' Scott said. He stopped when the engine of Parris's snowmobile quit.

The machine was a Silver Streak, with a battery starter and no other means of kicking it over. It did not take Parris long to establish that the battery had failed.

'Can I start it by towing you?' Scott asked.

'Not this model.' Parris began to put the protective cover over the machine. 'My trailer won't fit your hitch, so we'll have to use rope.'

Using nylon rope, they attached the trailer bar as close to the hitch as possible. 'You can ride back there,' Parris told Renfrow. 'I'm not even going to look around, so if you fall out, that's just your tough luck.'

Now it was night. Scott kept wiping snow from the headlight as they went slowly down the trail, with the trailer swinging from side to side on its make-shift hitch.

He drove across the sloping place and stopped. His voice seemed to die quickly as he called into the blast of snow and wind. 'Lassie! Lassie!'

Then, wallowing through the snow at the top of the cliff, he tried to see below with the aid of his flashlight, but the beam was lost amid whirling snow-flakes.

'We must have missed them somehow on the way in,' Renfrow said. 'By now they're probably back at the highway with the jeeps.'

'I don't know how we could have missed them,'

Parris growled. 'That Chinook is as big as a horse.'

Scott did not know what to think. His theory that Lassie had jumped from the trailer at this point now seemed no good at all. But why would she leave the beaten trail? Chinook must have found her, but now they both had disappeared.

'Say the word, and I'll get my snowshoes from the jeep, and I'll go with you anywhere you think we ought to look for them,' Parris said.

It was foolish to go by night into the storm on an aimless search, Scott knew. He had two hopes. First, that the dogs would be at the jeeps. Second, that Chinook, snow-wise by heritage, would get Lassie through the night, in case they were lost in the snow.

The dogs were not at the highway.

'Why don't you go on into town?' Scott said. 'I'll stick around for a while.'

'So will I.' Parris sent Renfrow down the highway with his jeep and trailer.

With the engine running and the heater going, the two men waited in Scott's jeep. They both fell sound asleep. Sometime later Scott woke with a start, having dreamed that Lassie was jumping against the door and barking to be let in.

When he opened the door, he saw nothing but the storm. Parris roused groggily when a bitter blast of cold struck him. 'Man, we're stupid, sleeping with that engine running,' he mumbled.

They had been there for over an hour. There was nothing more they could do that night towards finding Lassie and Chinook.

Sleeping in the snow beside Chinook, Lassie thought she heard Scott calling her name. It was a very faint, faraway sound, not enough to rouse her completely from exhaustion. She whined a little in her sleep and snuggled closer to Chinook's warmth.

At daylight Chinook surged up and shook himself. He nosed at Lassie, urging her to rise. The husky's incredible energy was at full peak again. He was ready to push straight through to safety, over there where they could hear the snowplough on the highway.

Lassie was game, but fighting through the snow again was a dreary prospect.

The storm had ended. It was much colder than the day before, and the wind was blowing snow in winding sheets.

For a while Lassie made good progress following Chinook, but the tremendous effort soon began to wear her down. He wallowed and ploughed and went by sheer brute power that seemed inexhaustible.

Though he was breaking trail the track he left was loose and shifting, and sometimes snow from the top caved into it in huge, powdery blobs.

Lassie had to move in desperate lunges, a few feet at a time, and then she had to rest.

Taking the direct route, Chinook started up a steep, timbered ridge. It was too much for Lassie. Chinook came wallowing back to her, as if to demonstrate how simple it was.

After a while he got the idea and continued on a downhill grade, but even that was beginning to be too much for Lassie. She had to rest longer and longer between each effort.

And then there came a time when, her strength sapped by the cold and the terrible struggle, she could go no farther, in spite of Chinook's help.

Chinook continued to go out and then return to her, whining anxiously. In an hour he could have been trotting down the highway. He went out, one time, clear to the end of the ridge and into a little saddle.

From there the sounds of the cars were loud, and it was not very far to the highway. But then he went back to Lassie. She was curled up in the snow, shivering.

Chinook licked her face, and then lay down beside her. The howling wind began to drift fine snow across them.

Chapter 11

SNOWSHOES

In Gateway the promise of a bright, clear day was in the air when Scott went to the district ranger's office long before regular opening hours. While it looked like a pleasant day in the valley, the whole Menzies Range was obscured by blowing snow.

Pete was on the phone talking to Sheriff Briscoe. 'He just came in, Chip. I'll let you know in a few minutes.' He hung up and turned to face Scott.

'The word sure gets around fast. The sheriff says he's had nothing but calls from people who want to go out with us to find Lassie and Chinook. Now, the question is, how many do we want?'

'I'll tell you one thing: we want only men who can get around on snowshoes. No snowmobile is going to move very far away from that logging road.'

'Ten men?'

Scott nodded. 'That's plenty.'

'You and Tommy and I are three. He's over at the garage getting the Rockets serviced and checked.'

'Parris will go.'

'Good. Jerry Wayne called a minute ago, and Pettigrew said he wanted to go. I told him we'd have enough, but he insisted.'

'How's Ted this morning?'

'A busted leg. That seems to be it. That's what comes of being young and lucky – *and* having Lassie poking around in a place where logic said no one would be.'

They made their plans, and then Pete called the sheriff, who complained that newsmen were giving him a fit. He had four of them in his office at the moment, waiting to go out with the search party.

A snowmobile from the ski course was just coming out on the logging road when Scott and Pete parked in the wide place, with six other vehicles behind them.

The two young men on the snowmobile said they had gone to look at the slide area and had discovered that a second slide had run, this time farther to the north than the first one.

Scott and Parris looked at each other grimly. The night before, when they had gone back to the slide area, they had not been able to see clear across it. Now they could not say whether or not the second slide had run before or after they were there.

There was a possibility that Lassie and Chinook had returned to the area and had been buried by that second snowslide.

The thought made Scott sick inside, but he stuck to his plan. He and Pete were going to act on Scott's hunch that Lassie had jumped from the trailer at the sloping place.

Tommy Thompson would be in charge of the searchers who would cruise slowly along the old road, looking for marks to indicate where the dogs had left the trail.

Renfrow and another man were going to the slide

area with a new battery for Parris's snowmobile. As far as possible, they would check in that vicinity.

The different groups would keep in touch with each other by radio. If none of them turned up any sign of the dogs by the time they had searched carefully close to the trail, then they would make a sweep downhill, on snowshoes, clear to the ski course.

Instead of the ten searchers Pete and Scott had planned on, there were twenty-one, plus five men from TV, radio and newspapers, who sensed considerable human-interest potential in the story of a dog rescuing a boy, then being lost herself.

Sheriff Briscoe arrived while Scott and Pete were detailing plans. With unconcealed dislike for the freezing blasts of wind and snow, the sheriff drew Scott aside at the first opportunity.

'Try to screen out anyone who's a dub on snowshoes, will you? We sure don't want to have a man lost or crippled out in this mess.'

'We're doing our best,' Scott said.

'I'll go back to the ski course. The dogs just might make it into there.'

Parris decided to stick with Scott and Pete.

The well-beaten track of the day before was now half full in places, with slanting banks of windblown snow. Though the ski course snowmobile had gone up and down the road only a short time before, Scott found himself churning through powder that rose in clouds to blow back into his face.

Near the cliff, he and Parris managed to get their machines far enough to one side to leave passing room for others.

While he was strapping on his snowshoes, Scott felt the bite of cold on his ungloved hands. It was at least twenty degrees colder than the day before, he thought, and the wind made it worse.

They got their packs on and snowshoed down a steep slope and around to the base of the cliff.

So sure was Scott that his hunch about Lassie's jumping from the trailer was right that he now felt jolted when he saw no evidence at all to support his theory.

Of course, it had snowed all night, and the wind had blown.

'I think you've figured it right,' Parris said. 'The cliff is about the only place where we could have lost her.'

'She'd have to go downhill,' Pete said.

Snow was blowing in streamers from the trees below. The thirty inches of fresh fall made heavy going for men on webs. They sank in at every step, then had to lift their feet high to make the next step.

For a while they followed the trees, looking under them for some sign that had not been covered.

The sheriff called from the ski course. 'No luck down here. How are you fellows doing?'

Scott had to fumble the stiff cover off the radio he was carrying. He was one of the last to answer, and his reply was the same as those from the other searchers.

'Nothing, so far.'

With the wind driving snow against his parka, he put the radio away and looked bleakly at the frozen scene.

If she *was* still alive, Lassie could not last much longer in this kind of cold. A husky could make it, yes, and come out strong.

And that was the only hope – that Chinook had stayed with Lassie.

One by one the calls came in. Those along the

trail had found nothing. They were now going to spread out for a sweep towards the ski course, and that would be blind searching.

Scott and his companions adjusted their search. They moved fifty yards apart and went on slowly, looking under each tree they passed.

Then, almost miraculously, something caught Scott's eye. Stooping to peer under boughs in a thicket, he saw strands of greyish hair caught on a twig. He had to take his snowshoes off and crawl under the limbs to reach the find.

Then, after he had the hairs in his hand, he could not identify them. His first thought, of course, had been that they were Lassie's. He called to his companions to come and have a look.

'I'd say that those came from Chinook,' Parris said. 'See the dark tips?'

Pete frowned. 'I'm no expert on fur.'

'If they were here, there has to be a track leading away.' Scott strapped on just one snowshoe.

Standing on one web, they each used their other one to dig in a circle around the tree. There was a track that Lassie and Chinook had made, but they dug through it. It had been made in fresh snow, and it had been filled so quickly afterwards that there were no crusted edges to define it, and so they did not know that they were on the right track.

As they went on, searching blindly, the radio calls continued to report no sign of the dogs.

'Still negative here,' Sheriff Briscoe said. 'It's twenty-three degrees below zero. They've shut the lifts down. Not even the ski idiots can take it now. How are you doing, Unit one-two-three-six?'

'We're still going,' Scott said.

'I'm afraid you'll have to call it off before long.'

'He's in the lodge, drinking coffee, warm as toast,' Pete said bitterly.

'He may be warm, but he's also right,' Scott said. There was a limit to human endurance, and Scott knew that he himself was nearing that limit.

Twenty-three degrees below zero was no great problem for outdoor men properly dressed, but the wind was making the effective cold possibly fifty degrees lower. And the altitude, too, was another crippling factor.

The facts could not be denied. Before long they would have to quit.

Sometime later Parris called excitedly from a little saddle, where he had veered off at a right angle to scan the country. Scott and Pete had gone farther east, but now they climbed up to Parris.

It was there, a trail between the rocks where an animal had smashed the snow down. The edges of it were crusted, so it must have been made after the storm stopped and the cold set in.

Just faintly the track was outlined on the surface of the snow to the west, showing that the dogs – it must have been the dogs, Scott thought – had come along the side of the ridge. It was logical to assume that they had crossed the saddle and gone on downhill.

Scott called the other searchers and gave the news. Some of them were already headed for the ski lodge, as fast they could go. Jerry Wayne said the group with him would come right over to help run out the trail.

Scott and his companions found no sign of tracks below the saddle. 'There's something odd about this,' Parris said, looking at the unbroken snow. 'I know those tracks above us were made after the snow stopped, but why aren't there marks down here?'

'The wind,' Pete said.

With their backs to the freezing gusts, they talked it over. The dogs had reached the saddle. From there it was not to far to the highway. Surely they would have continued downhill.

The searchers spread out and started down the slope.

A few moments later a long-drawn howl drifted across the frozen wilderness. It ended while the searchers were still turning their heads, unsure of the direction from which it had come.

At first Scott though it had come from somewhere near the highway, but then he did not know. They waited for it to come again, but all they heard was the roar of the wind and the grinding rumble of a truck.

Although they knew where the truck was, the noise of its engine seemed to be coming from the mountains behind them.

Scott untied his parka hood and threw it back. He turned and snowshoed up the steep hill to the saddle, then stood there waiting.

The call came again. It started low, and then it ran on into an extended, mournful howl that was enough to make a man's hair stand on end.

Chinook! This time Scott was sure of the direction. 'He's back of us!' He waved for his companions to join him.

The husky came plunging to meet them when they were still a hundred yards from where Lassie lay under the snow, with just an opening at her muzzle for breathing.

Scott brushed the snow from her. She whined a feeble welcome as he felt her legs and put his hand against her side to feel her heartbeat.

'I think she's all right. Let's get her out of here as fast as we can.'

They wrapped her in a blanket and put her on another blanket. Chinook was so happy to see them that he became a nuisance. One instant he was licking Lassie's face, and the next he was bumping against someone's legs.

He stepped on one of Parris's snowshoes and tripped Parris headlong into the snow. 'Watch it, you overgrown moose!' Parris yelled.

Pete called the other searchers. 'We've found the dogs. We'll be carrying Lassie. Our probable point of entry to the highway: one mile and a half below the logging road.'

Sheriff Briscoe's voice came in immediately. 'Dr Inman says he'll meet you there with his station wagon. How is Lassie?'

'Fair condition, we think.'

Scott took the back end of the blanket, with Pete and Parris each on a front corner. Seemingly untired, Chinook went on ahead of them.

Scott had not put his parka hood up, and by the time they reached the saddle, his ears were freezing. They stopped there for a moment to let him adjust the hood.

Though they were fired up with new energy because their mission was almost accomplished, they were having a hard time walking so close together. Since he was at the apex of the triangle, Scott could not go in the tracks his companions were making. The outside half of each snowshoe came down where the two other men had stepped, while the inside half was on unbroken snow. He was sinking in unevenly, stumbling.

Pete thought he could do better in back, but after he exchanged positions with Scott, he, too, began to lurch and stumble.

'Put her down,' Parris said.

They let Lassie down on the snow. Parris wrapped the bottom blanket around her, on top of the first one, leaving only her head exposed, and then he picked her up in his arms and walked away.

They took turns carrying her. Still out in front of them, waiting at times for them to catch up, was the tireless Chinook.

'That's monster's energy is disgusting,' Scott said. 'Look at him go.'

'Where was he when we passed that ridge?' Pete said. 'Buried in the snow beside Lassie?'

'He must have been,' Scott said. 'When I first got there, there was a cavity that looked as if he had erupted straight up from the snow.'

They were about halfway to the road when Jerry Wayne and three other men caught up with them. They all took turns carrying Lassie.

Just before they reached the steep bank that led down to the highway, Wayne gave Scott a quiet look and said, 'You know something? We can't blame the Snow Dust Twins for these last two days. They're the ones who almost got it, but there're about a hundred and seventy of us who share the blame.'

Scott made no comment, but Parris overheard Wayne's words and said, 'That's right, Jerry.'

If something good came out of the ordeal of the past two days, that would be fine, Scott told himself. But it was surely the hard way to get things done.

Scott was carrying Lassie when the rescue party, half sliding, half falling, plunged down a snowy bank and reached the highway.

The sheriff and Dr Inman were waiting beside a station wagon, and three newsmen were on the scene. They had been taking pictures ever since the rescue party had come in sight.

Dr Inman took Lassie from Scott and put her on blankets in the warm station wagon. 'I've already called the animal hospital, Scott. I assumed that you'd want to take her there.'

'Thanks.' Scott was suddenly so tired that all he wanted to do was sit down.

'Go ahead,' Pete said. 'We'll stick around to be sure that everyone gets out of the woods.' He grabbed Chinook around the neck to keep him from getting into the station wagon with Lassie and Scott.

The big husky pulled Pete off his feet, but he held on, and the newsmen were quick to take pictures of him sprawled at the edge of the highway with his arms around Chinook.

As the station wagon pulled away, Lassie raised her head and looked back, as if questioning the act of leaving Chinook behind.

Scott stroked her head gently. 'He's all right, Lassie, and you're going to be fine.'

'After what she did for that Pettigrew boy, I'll take her on as a patient any old time,' Dr Inman said.

Chapter 12

A NEW START

Dr Aaron Waddell was a brisk young man with a serious expression and a sharp way of eyeing a person while he was speaking. He put Lassie on the examination table in the animal hospital and began a thorough examination.

'About sixteen hours out in the snow, eh? Hmmm! I guess you know that collies aren't designed for that sort of work.'

Dr Inman and Scott looked at each other. 'She wasn't there by anyone's choice,' Dr Inman said, attempting to explain the situation.

'Uh-huh, uh-huh.' Dr Waddell listened to Lassie's lungs with a stethoscope. She was beginning to pant a little in the heat of the room. 'Hmmm! There doesn't seem to be any congestion in the lungs.'

After ten minutes of careful checking, Dr Waddell said cautiously, 'She's in pretty good condition, considering. I'd like to keep her under observation, though, at least until sometime tomorrow.'

For all his brisk, preoccupied manner, there was a gleam of genuine warmth in the vet's eyes as he ran his hand along Lassie's neck. 'Collies haven't got the greatest noses in the world, you know, but still she found Ted Pettigrew.'

'She found him,' Scott said. He would be haunted at times by the fact that he and the rest of the rescue party on the snowslide had given up and were walking away at the time Lassie and Chinook began to bark excitedly.

'No matter how long she has to stay here, there will be no charge for this girl,' Dr Waddell said. 'How about Pettigrew's husky? How did he come through it?'

'Like a hero,' Dr Inman said. 'The last I saw of him, he had jumped up on the hood of a jeep, and the photographers were taking pictures of him.'

Driving Scott to his motel, Dr Inman said, 'The sheriff told me how you've been trying to bring some kind of voluntary control to the snowmobile situation. Many years ago we had the same kind of chaos in skiing.

'Because I saw so many injuries that were badly treated by untrained first-aid people or, in a lot of cases, by just anyone who was first at the scene of a skiing accident, I became interested in the National Ski Patrol. I've been with the organisation for a long time.

'We had our troubles, I can tell you, injecting safety principles into a growing sport. You're up against the same thing now in snowmobiling. I'll be at the ski lodge for another week, Scott, so if there's any way I can help you with your programme, just let me know.'

'Thanks. I may just call on you for help.'

Scott heard the phone ringing while he was unlocking the door to his motel room. A national press service wanted to know all about Lassie.

He was on his way to the shower when a TV station

called. He had barely hung up when he got another call from the regional forester.

'How's that boy that Lassie saved getting along?'

'Fine, the last I heard.'

'And Lassie?'

'I think she'll be all right.'

'Good! Won't the whole incident help you quite a bit with your work down there?'

'Look, chief, I didn't start that snowslide and toss the boy into it.'

'I realise that, Scott! But – ' The regional forester paused. 'You sound a little tired. Did you just now get in?'

'Yeah. And now I'm trying to take a shower.'

'Go ahead. Soak up some heat. I'll call you tomorrow.'

Scott pushed the switch down and made a call of his own, before someone else could get to him. He phoned the hospital and asked about Ted Pettigrew. The answer was 'Condition good.'

Again he started towards the shower. The phone tried to call him back, but this time he let it ring. Afterwards he called the office and told the motel owner to direct all inquiries about Lassie and the snowslide to the sheriff's office.

After all, Chip Briscoe had not been out in the snow for the best part of two days and nights; he had deputies who could supply newsmen and others with information.

Good relations between the press and the Forest Service were quite vital, Scott knew, and he had always done his best to uphold his end of things. But at the moment, good relations with a bed were all he had in mind.

* * *

It was after dark when low voices outside his door awakened him. He might have disregarded pounding on the door, but the noise of a quiet argument outside brought him out of bed. He had slept long enough anyway, he thought, and now he was getting hungry.

When he opened the door, a blunt muzzle poked in, and Chinook came crowding into the room. Bob Pettigrew and Benny were standing outside, with half guilty expressions on their faces.

'Come in,' Scott said, 'before that draught freezes my legs.'

'We knocked, and then decided you were asleep, and we thought maybe we ought to beat it, and Benny said – '

'I was just ready to get up, anyway. How's Ted?'

'Pretty good,' Bob said. 'We just came from the hospital. They're going to set his leg tomorrow.'

Chinook was sniffing around where Lassie had slept. 'She isn't around here, dumbhead!' Bob said. 'You know she's out at Doc Waddell's.' He looked at Scott. 'We were there, too. Doc let us see Lassie for a minute. He said she was starting to develop a cold, but he gave her a shot. She'll be all right, won't she?'

'I hope so. What did Ted have to say about the snowslide?' Scott was sitting on the edge of his bed. He was warm and rested, and it seemed like a long time ago that he had seen the cornice breaking above two blue Skimmers.

'He unloaded just about the time he saw he was going to bury his skis in that trench,' Bob said. 'He said he was running up the trail towards the north side, with old Chinook scooting ahead of him, and then they both got knocked end over end.

'He said he kept trying to stomp and claw to keep

on top, but it just kept rolling him under. All the time he was jammed up in that mess of snow and branches, he said he was sure we would find him, but he was worrying about what happened to me and Benny.

'He remembered hearing the dogs barking, and after that he doesn't remember anything until he was in the ambulance with Dad and Dr Inman.'

Scott nodded slowly. 'How would you two like to be buried the way he was?'

'You don't have to tell us,' Benny said. 'We've learned our lesson. My dad didn't get mad, but by the time he got through talking to me, I wished I'd never heard of a snowmobile.'

'My dad had a few things to say, too,' Bob said. 'He blamed himself for a lot of it. He knew we'd been sneaking the pickup on to back roads to get to the mountains. Of course, Benny or somebody else always drove us when we went very far on the highway, but that's all done, for good, now.'

'Fine!' Scott said. 'You may live to be old snowmobilers. Now get out of here so I can shave and dress. I'm hungry as a bear.'

'Chinook ate three cans of dog food,' Benny said.

Scott laughed and gave Chinook a friendly whack. 'I think I'll try a steak, myself.'

Going out, the boys stalled in the doorway.

'My dad says he's going to do everything he can to get your doggoned old clubs organised,' Bob said.

'I'm glad to hear that, but they won't be *my* clubs, you know.'

'Well, it was your idea.'

'Close that door before you freeze me!'

'How can you freeze down here? Up there in the mountains, where it was really cold – '

'Goodbye! I'll see you guys later.'

There was a different attitude this time as snowmobilers and those interested in the sport crowded into Community Hall. Before, many had come with a hostile, show-me attitude, ready to resist what they considered to be interference in their private affairs. Now it was the snowmobilers themselves who had called the meeting.

Scott and Pete and Sheriff Briscoe took chairs in the back row. Fully recovered, Lassie watched with interest as people poured into the room. When the meeting began, she lay down and went to sleep.

Barbara Vogel made the report for the committee that had been appointed to look into the matter of forming clubs.

'I think you'll agree that what happened last week up there on Elk Pass presents the case for our taking responsibility for the sport, and it does it much better than any of us can put into words.' She went on to detail plans for three snowmobile clubs, with safety rules and codes of behaviour.

Sheriff Briscoe smiled as the talk from the floor favoured the committee's recommendations. 'They just discovered everything that we tried to pound into their heads at the last meeting. I think they would have come around to it in time, anyway, but that snowslide was a pretty good jab with a sharp stick.' The sheriff chuckled. 'You didn't start that slide, did you, Scott?'

'Yep! I did it with a ping-pong ball.'

Jerry Wayne and Pettigrew were two of the first to throw their weight behind the club idea. After that, Scott had no doubts that the plans would go ahead full speed.

It was a great step. Not every problem would be solved just because there were clubs. There would always be those few who acted irresponsibly. But the sport would be under the control of the snowmobilers themselves, and that was the most effective way to bring order and safety to it.

Shortly before the meeting broke up, Pettigrew said, 'I don't know what names will be proposed for the clubs, but I'm going to have two decals on my snowmobile from now on.

'I'm sure you all know, or at least you've heard plenty about, the two who are going to be pictured on those decals. I now propose them for lifetime honorary membership in our groups.'

Pettigrew paused and looked around, and then he said, 'Lassie and Shinook!'

Lassie awakened when she heard her name, and then she sat up and barked as tremendous applause rocked the room.

TARGET STORY BOOKS

Fantasy And General Fiction

	Elisabeth Beresford		
101537	AWKWARD MAGIC	(illus)	60p
10479X	SEA-GREEN MAGIC	(illus)	60p
101618	TRAVELLING MAGIC	(illus)	60p
	Eileen Dunlop		
119142	ROBINSHEUGH	(illus)	60p
	Maria Gripe		
112288	THE GLASSBLOWER'S CHILDREN	(illus)	45p
	Joyce Nicholson		
117891	FREEDOM FOR PRISCILLA		70p
	Hilary Seton		
106989	THE HUMBLES	(illus)	50p
109112	THE NOEL STREATFEILD CHRISTMAS HOLIDAY BOOK	(illus)	60p
109031	THE NOEL STREATFEILD EASTER HOLIDAY BOOK	(illus)	60p
105249	THE NOEL STREATFEILD SUMMER HOLIDAY BOOK	(illus)	50p

Humour

	Eleanor Estes		
107519	THE WITCH FAMILY	(illus)	50p
	Felice Holman		
11762X	THE WITCH ON THE CORNER	(illus)	50p
	Spike Milligan		
105672	BADJELLY THE WITCH	(illus)	60p
109546	DIP THE PUPPY	(illus)	60p
	Christine Nostlinger		
107438	THE CUCUMBER KING	(illus)	45p
	Mary Rogers		
119223	A BILLION FOR BORIS		60p

0426

Film And TV Tie-ins

	Kathleen N. Daly		
200187	RAGGEDY ANN AND ANDY	(Colour illus)	75p ♦
	John Ryder Hall		
11826X	SINBAD AND THE EYE OF THE TIGER		70p* ♦
	John Lucarotti		
11535X	OPERATION PATCH		45p
	Pat Sandys		
119495	THE PAPER LADS		60p ♦
	Alison Thomas		
115511	BENJI		40p

†For sale in Britain and Ireland only.
*Not for sale in Canada.
♦ Film & T.V. tie-ins.

TARGET NON-FICTION

General Non-fiction And biography

108906	Elizabeth Gundrey THE SUMMER BOOK	(illus)	45p
113594	Larry Kettelkamp INVESTIGATING UFOs	(illus)	50p
114396	Carey Miller THE TARGET BOOK OF FATE & FORTUNE	(illus)	50p
10823X	Christopher Reynolds CREATURES OF THE BAY	(illus)	50p
112369	David Shaw CRAFTS FOR GIRLS	(illus)	50p

Quiz And Games

102843	Nicola Davies THE TARGET BOOK OF FUN AND GAMES	(illus)	50p
10532X	THE 2nd TARGET BOOK OF FUN AND GAMES	(illus)	50p
109465	THE 3rd TARGET BOOK OF FUN AND GAMES	(illus)	50p
115198	THE TARGET BOOK OF JOKES		40p
116232	Harry Baron THE TARGET BOOK OF MAGIC	(illus)	70p
118340	G. J. B. Laverty THE TARGET BOOK OF CROSSWORDS FOR FUN		50p
117115	D. & C. Power THE TARGET BOOK OF PICTURE PUZZLES		40p
118855	Fred Reinfeld THE TARGET BOOK OF CHESS	(illus)	60p

†For sale in Britain and Ireland only.
*Not for sale in Canada.
♦ Film & T.V. tie-ins.

TARGET STORY BOOKS

'Doctor Who'

No.	Title			Price
200020	DOCTOR WHO DISCOVERS PREHISTORIC ANIMALS	(NF)	(illus)	75p
200039	DOCTOR WHO DISCOVERS SPACE TRAVEL	(NF)	(illus)	75p
200047	DOCTOR WHO DISCOVERS STRANGE AND MYSTERIOUS CREATURES	(NF)	(illus)	75p
20008X	DOCTOR WHO DISCOVERS THE STORY OF EARLY MAN	(NF)	(illus)	75p
200136	DOCTOR WHO DISCOVERS THE CONQUERORS	(NF)	(illus)	75p
116313	Ian Marter DOCTOR WHO AND THE ARK IN SPACE			50p
116747	Terrance Dicks DOCTOR WHO AND THE BRAIN OF MORBIUS			50p*
110250	Terrance Dicks DOCTOR WHO AND THE CARNIVAL OF MONSTERS			50p
11471X	Malcolm Hulke DOCTOR WHO AND THE CAVE MONSTERS			60p
117034	Terrance Dicks DOCTOR WHO AND THE CLAWS OF AXOS			50p*
113160	David Whitaker DOCTOR WHO AND THE CRUSADERS		(illus)	60p
114981	Brian Hayles DOCTOR WHO AND THE CURSE OF PELADON			60p
114639	Gerry Davis DOCTOR WHO AND THE CYBERMEN			60p
113322	Barry Letts DOCTOR WHO AND THE DAEMONS		(illus)	40p
101103	David Whitaker DOCTOR WHO AND THE DALEKS			60p
11244X	Terrance Dicks DOCTOR WHO AND THE DALEK INVASION OF EARTH			[illegible]
119657	Terrance Dicks DOCTOR WHO AND THE DEA[illegible]			[illegible]
200063	Terrance Dicks DOCTOR WHO AND THE FA[illegible] OF EVIL			[illegible]
112601	Terrance Dicks DOCTOR WHO AND THE G[illegible] OF THE DALEKS			[illegible]

†For sale i[illegible]

Wyndham Books are obtainable from many booksellers and newsagents. If you have any difficulty please send purchase price plus postage on the scale below to:

Wyndham Cash Sales:
P O Box 11,
Falmouth,
Cornwall.

or

Star Book Service:
G P O Box 29,
Douglas,
Isle of Man,
British Isles.

While every effort is made to keep prices low, it is sometimes necessary to increase prices at short notice. Wyndham Books reserve the right to show new retail prices on covers which may differ from those advertised in the text or elsewhere.

Postage and Packing Rate

UK

22p for the first book plus 10p per copy for each additional book ordered to a maximum charge of 82p.

BFPO and Eire

22p for the first book, plus 10p per copy for the next 6 books and thereafter 4p per book.

book and 10p per copy for each additional

subject to Post Office charge fluctua-